"I was just sure a man thoughtful enough to join the Handyman Ministry would understand how much a ranch trip could mean to at-risk town kids," Rainy said.

So it was a cheap shot. Rainy had no remorse. She was accustomed to pushing when it came to getting things for foster children.

Nate leaned back in his chair, staring at her with exasperation. "You don't give up, do you?"

A tiny smile tickled Rainy's lips. "Never. Not when it comes to my kids."

The cowboy across from her raised his hands in surrender. "Okay, they can come to my ranch."

He was ready to cut and run like a wild horse. Better grab the opportunity while it was knocking.

Books by Linda Goodnight

Love Inspired

In the Spirit of…Christmas
A Very Special Delivery
***A Season for Grace*
**A Touch of Grace
***The Heart of Grace*
Missionary Daddy
A Time to Heal
Home to Crossroads Ranch

**The Brothers' Bond

LINDA GOODNIGHT

Winner of the 2007 RITA® Award for excellence in inspirational fiction, Linda Goodnight has also won the Booksellers' Best, ACFW Book of the Year, and a Reviewers' Choice Award from *Romantic Times BOOKreviews*. Linda has appeared on the Christian bestseller list and her romance novels have been translated into more than a dozen languages. Active in orphan ministry, this former nurse and teacher enjoys writing fiction that carries a message of hope and light in a sometimes dark world. She and husband Gene live in Oklahoma. Readers can write to her at linda@lindagoodnight.com, or c/o Steeple Hill Books, 233 Broadway, Suite 1001, New York, NY 10279.

Home to Crossroads Ranch
Linda Goodnight

Steeple
Hill®

Published by Steeple Hill Books™

STEEPLE HILL BOOKS

Steeple
Hill®

ISBN-13: 978-0-373-87521-4
ISBN-10:   0-373-87521-5

HOME TO CROSSROADS RANCH

Printed in U.S.A.

For by grace you have been saved through faith;
and that not of yourselves: it is the gift of God;
not of works, lest any man should boast.

—*Ephesians* 2:8–9

Chapter One

Nate Del Rio heard screams the minute he stepped out of his Super Crew Cab and started up the flower-lined sidewalk leading to Rainy Jernagen's house. He double-checked the address scribbled on the back of a bill for horse feed. Sure enough, this was the place.

Adjusting his Stetson against a gust of March wind, he rang the doorbell expecting the noise to subside. It didn't.

Somewhere inside the modest, tidy-looking brick house at least two kids were screaming their heads off in what sounded to his experienced ears like fits of temper. A television blasted out Saturday-morning cartoons.

He punched the doorbell again. Instead of the expected *ding-dong,* a raucous alternative Christian rock band added a few more decibels to the noise level.

Nate shifted the toolbox to his opposite hand and considered running for his life while he had the chance.

Too late. The bright red door whipped open. Nate's mouth fell open with it.

When the men's ministry coordinator from Bible Fellowship had called him, he'd somehow gotten the impression that he was coming to help a little old schoolteacher. In his mind, that meant the kind who only drove to school and church and had a big, fat cat.

Not so. The woman standing before him with taffy-blond hair sprouting out from a disheveled ponytail couldn't possibly be any older than his thirty-one years. A big blotch of something purple stained the front of her white sweatshirt, and she was barefoot. Plus, she had a crying baby on each hip and a little red-haired girl hanging on one leg, bawling like a sick calf. And there wasn't a cat in sight.

What had he gotten himself into?

"May I help you?" she asked over the racket. Her blue-gray eyes were a little too unfocused and bewildered for his comfort.

Raising his voice, he asked, "Are you Ms. Jernagen?"

"Yes," she said cautiously. "I'm Rainy Jernagen. And you are…?"

"Nate Del Rio."

She blinked, uncomprehending, all the while jiggling both babies up and down. One grabbed a hunk of her hair. She flinched, her head angling to one side, as she said, still cautiously, "Okaaay."

Nate reached out and untwined the baby's sticky fingers.

A relieved smile rewarded him. "Thanks. Is there something I can help you with?"

He hefted the red toolbox to chest level so she could see it. "From the Handyman Ministry. Jack Martin called. Said you had a washer problem."

Understanding dawned. "Oh my goodness. Yes. I'm so sorry. You aren't what I expected. Please forgive me."

She wasn't what he expected, either. Not in the least. Young and with a houseful of kids. He suppressed a shiver. Kids, even grown ones, could drive a person to distraction. He should know. His adult sister and brother were, at this moment, making his life as miserable as possible. The worst part was they did it all the time. Only this morning his sister Janine had finally packed up and gone back to Sal, giving Nate a few days' reprieve.

"Come in, come in," the woman was saying. "It's been a crazy morning, what with the babies showing up at 3 a.m. and Katie having a sick stomach. Then while I was doing the laundry, the washing machine went crazy. Water everywhere." She jerked her chin toward the inside of the house. "You're truly a godsend."

He wasn't so sure about that, but he'd signed up for his church's ministry to help single women and the elderly with those pesky little handyman chores like oil changes and leaky faucets. Most of his visits had been to older ladies who plied him with sweet tea and jars of homemade jam and talked about the good old days while he replaced a fuse or unstopped the sink. And their houses had been quiet. Real quiet.

Rainy Jernagen stepped back, motioning him in, and Nate very cautiously entered a room that should have had flashing red lights and a Danger Zone sign.

Toys littered the living room like it was Christmas morning. An overturned cereal bowl flowed milk onto a coffee table. Next to a playpen crowding one wall, a green package belched out disposable diapers. Similarly, baby clothes were strewn, along with a couple of kids, on the couch and floor. In a word, the place was a wreck.

"The washer is back this way behind the kitchen. Watch your step. It's slippery."

More than slippery. Nate kicked his way through the living room and the kitchen area. Though the kitchen actually appeared much tidier than the rest, he still caught the slow seepage of water coming from somewhere beyond the wall. The shine of liquid glistening on beige tile led them straight to the utility room.

"I turned the faucets off behind the washer when this first

started, but a tubful still managed to pump out onto the floor."
She hoisted the babies higher on her hip and spoke to a young
boy sitting on the floor. "Joshua, get out of those suds."

"But they're pretty, Miss Rainy." The brown-haired boy
with bright blue eyes grinned up at her, extending a handful
of bubbles. Light reflected off each droplet. "See the
rainbows? There's always a rainbow, like you said. A rainbow
behind the rain."

Rainy smiled at the child. "Yes, there is. But right now,
Mr. Del Rio needs to get in here to fix the washer. It's a little
crowded for all of us." She was right about that. The space
was no bigger than a small bathroom. "Can I get you to take
the babies to the playpen while I show him around?"

"I'll take them, Miss Rainy." An older boy with a serious
face and brown plastic glasses entered the room. Treading
carefully, he came forward and took both babies, holding
them against his slight chest. Another child appeared behind
him, this one a girl with very blond hair and eyes the exact
blue of the boy she'd called Joshua. How many children did
this woman have, anyway? Six?

A heavy, smothery feeling pressed against his airway. Six
kids?

Before he could dwell on that disturbing thought, a scream
of sonic proportions rent the soap-fragrant air. He whipped
around, ready to protect and defend.

The little blond girl and the redhead were going at it.

"It's mine." Blondie tugged hard on a doll.

"It's mine. Will said so." To add emphasis to her demand,
the redhead screamed bloody murder. "Miss Rainy!"

About that time, Joshua decided to skate across the suds,
and slammed into the far wall next to a door that probably
opened into the garage. He grabbed his big toe and sent up
a howl. Water sloshed as Rainy rushed forward and gathered
him into her arms.

"Rainy!" Blondie screamed again.

"Rainy!" the redhead yelled.

Nate cast a glance at the garage exit and considered a fast escape.

Lord, I'm here to do a good thing. Can You help me out a little?

Rainy, her clothes now wet, somehow managed to take the doll from the fighting girls while snuggling Joshua against her side. The serious-looking boy stood in the doorway, a baby on each hip, taking in the chaos.

"Come on, Emma," he said to Blondie. "I'll make you some chocolate milk." So they went, slip-sliding out of the flooded room.

Four down, two to go.

Nate clunked his toolbox onto the washer and tried to ignore the chaos. Not an easy task, but one he'd learned to deal with as a boy. As an adult, he did everything possible to avoid this kind of madness. The Lord had a sense of humor sending him to this particular house.

"I apologize, Mr. Del Rio," Rainy said, shoving at the wads of hair that hung around her face like Spanish moss.

"Call me Nate. I'm not that much older than you." Being the longtime patriarch of his family, he might feel seventy, but he wasn't.

"Okay, Nate. And I'm Rainy. Really, it's not usually this bad. I can't thank you enough for coming over. I tried to get a plumber, but today being Saturday…" She shrugged, letting the obvious go unsaid. No one could get a plumber on the weekend.

"No problem." He removed his white Stetson and placed it next to the toolbox. What was he supposed to say? That he loved wading through dirty soapsuds and listening to kids scream and cry? Not likely.

Rainy stood with an arm around each of the remaining

children—the rainbow boy and the redhead. Her look of embarrassment had him feeling sorry for her. All these kids and no man around to help. With this many, she'd never find another husband, he was sure of that. Who would willingly take on a boatload of kids?

After a minute, Rainy and the remaining pair left the room and he got to work. Wiggling the machine away from the wall wasn't easy. Even with all the water on the floor, a significant amount remained in the tub. This leftover liquid sloshed and gushed at regular intervals. In minutes, his boots were dark with moisture. No problem there. As a rancher, his boots were often dark with lots of things, the best of which was water.

On his haunches, he surveyed the back of the machine where hoses and cords and metal parts twined together like a nest of water moccasins.

As he investigated each hose in turn, he once more felt a presence in the room. Pivoting on his heels, he discovered the two boys squatting beside him, attention glued to the back of the washer. Blondie hovered in the background.

"A busted hose?" the oldest one asked, pushing up his glasses.

"Most likely."

"I coulda fixed it but Rainy wouldn't let me."

"That so?"

"Yeah. Maybe. If someone would show me."

Nate suppressed a smile. "What's your name?"

"Will. This here's my brother, Joshua." He yanked a thumb at the younger one. "He's nine. I'm eleven. My sister's Emma. She's seven. You go to Miss Rainy's church?"

"I do, but it's a big church. I don't think we've met before."

"She's nice. Most of the time. She never hits us or anything, and we've been here for six months."

It occurred to Nate then that these were not Rainy's

children. The kids called her Miss Rainy, not Mom, and according to Will they had not been here forever. But what was a young, single woman doing with all these kids? Foster care? Nah, they didn't let singles do that. Did they?

Rainy frantically tossed toys into a basket in an effort to clear up some of the mess. She never let things get like this. Of all the days to have a stranger come into her home. A young, nice-looking stranger at that.

Pausing with a stuffed bear against her cheek, she chuckled. The poor man looked as bewildered as if he'd walked into the *Twilight Zone.*

She'd had to call upon the Handyman Ministry before but her friendly rescuers had been older fatherly types, not a lanky young cowboy in starched jeans and boots with stubble on his chin and a dangerous set of dimples that split his cheeks like long parentheses. Killer dimples.

She tossed the bear into the basket and went for a sponge to soak up the coffee-table mess.

With dimples like that, Nate Del Rio was probably like every other guy she'd noticed in the last two years—married.

She heaved a heavy sigh and dabbed at the spilled milk. For years, she'd prayed for a godly husband, but the Lord didn't appear interested in her single, lonely status or in the fact that she wanted kids. Lots of kids. The dates she'd had never filled the bill and after a while, she'd given up the dating game entirely. It was too stressful anyway.

If she couldn't have a husband and kids, she'd settle for kids only.

But she wasn't dead, and Nate Del Rio was an attractive man.

She clicked off the blasting television and then handed each of the babies in the playpen a rattle. Precious little lambs. They looked so bewildered by this new, unfamiliar environment. As soon as she had a minute, she needed to hold and rock them, give them the comfort they craved and deserved.

With the TV off, the room had grown a little too quiet. She glanced into the bedroom to find Katie sprawled on the floor, coloring. Good. Maybe her stomachache was gone. Now, where were the others?

With another quick, reassuring glance at the babies, she headed for the laundry room. The sibling trio was naturally nosy, but they also hungered for attention from any obliging adult.

Sure enough, Joshua and Will were squatting in an inch of water, peppering Nate with questions. Seven-year-old Emma, the blond charmer, hung over the man's back, her slender arms looped around his neck like a small, friendly boa constrictor.

"Emma," Rainy said gently. "It's hard for Nate to work with you hanging on him. Why don't you and the boys come out of here and leave him alone?"

"But, Miss Rainy, he's teaching me how to change a hose so I can do it next time." Will's eyes were dead serious behind his glasses. That was the trouble with Will. He was too serious. He seldom laughed, didn't play like a normal kid and considered his younger siblings to be his responsibility. Even after six months of consistent, loving care, he hadn't loosened up. The boy needed a strong man in his life, one of the reasons Rainy worried about adopting him and his siblings, though she longed to do so. She could love and nurture, but she could never be a male role model. She could, however, expose him to good ones and pray that would be enough.

The cowboy handyman twisted his head in her direction. "He's a quick learner."

Rainy beamed as if the compliment was for her. She saw the flush of pleasure on Will's cheeks and decided she liked Nate Del Rio. "He is. Thanks."

She bent to unwind Emma from the man's neck. "This one

is a charmer, but also a pest at times." With a counselor and lots of prayers, they were working on Emma's weak personal boundaries. "Come on, Emma. I need help with the babies."

Emma came, but gazed longingly at the cowboy's back. "He's nice."

Rainy stood in the doorway for a minute, watching and listening to Nate's low voice explaining the great mysteries of washing machines to the two rapt boys. His patience with them solidified her conclusion that he had kids of his own.

She chided herself for being disappointed. She did not covet another woman's husband. She simply wanted one of her own.

"Is there anything you need before I go on about my business?" she asked.

Without turning, he shook his head. "Got all the help I need right now. Thanks."

She wasn't sure how he meant that, but she let it go and headed back to the disaster area that had once been her home.

By the time she'd set things to right, fed both babies and put them down for a nap, Katie had thrown up again. Wearily, she cleaned up the mess, took the child's temperature and debated calling the doctor. The last thing any of them needed was a virus spreading through the house.

Going to her bedroom to change the now disgusting sweat suit, she happened to glance in the mirror. The Wicked Witch of the West stared back.

Bags the size of carry-on luggage puffed beneath her eyes. Her hair shot out in every direction. She slapped at it. Had she combed it at all this morning?

With a growing sense of chagrin, she knew she hadn't. She had shoved the shoulder-length mass into a scrunchie in the wee hours of the morning when the social worker arrived with the babies. After that she never made it back to bed because Katie had started throwing up. Then the washer had sprung a leak and she'd been too busy to care about how she looked.

Horrid. She looked horrid. Horror-movie horrid.

No wonder the kids were crying. She was tempted to do the same.

Quickly yanking away the scrunchie along with a few hairs, Rainy ran a brush over her head and put the ponytail up again. Better.

She leaned into the mirror and grimaced. Makeup. Fast.

She dabbed a little concealer under each eye, mostly to no avail, stroked some mascara on thick lashes and added a hint of pink lip gloss. She was no beauty, but she normally tried to accent her best features, thick lashes and a tilted, full mouth. Today she'd settle for not frightening small children.

"Miss Rainy!"

This would have to do. Without a backward glance, she rushed toward the sound of Katie's voice.

The child lay on the couch where Rainy had left her, a pink Hello Kitty blanket up to her chin.

"What is it, punkin? Are you feeling sick again?"

"I want a Pop-Tart."

"Are you sure that's such a good idea? How about something gentle on your tummy first and then the Pop-Tart later."

A million russet freckles stood out on the sad, pale face. "Okay."

Rainy entered the kitchen as Nate Del Rio and the boys entered from the opposite end. Nate glanced up at her, surprise registering in his eyes.

"You look—" He seemed to catch himself, for which she would be eternally grateful, and said instead, "We're all finished. If you'll hand us a mop, we'll sop up some of the water for you."

"Oh, goodness no. Don't bother. I'll do the sopping up. You've done enough." She whipped toward the broom closet and took out a sponge mop. "Why don't you have a seat and let me get you some cookies and milk."

Those dimples of his activated. Killer dimples. Goodness.

"Cookies and milk? Sounds great. My breakfast wore off after the stop at Milly Jenkins's."

"Milly?" Rainy propped the mop against the wall, only to have it taken by Will, who disappeared into the laundry room with faithful Joshua by his side. "Doesn't she play the organ at church?"

"Yep. Nice lady. Her old Mercury needed new spark plugs."

Rainy took down two glasses and filled them with cold milk, then added milk to the ongoing grocery list posted on the fridge. "This ministry is a real blessing to people, Nate. I hope you men who volunteer realize that."

"It's a blessing to us, too," he said simply, and she liked him for the sentiment. Nice guy. No wonder some smart woman had snapped him up like the last chocolate truffle.

With a plate of yesterday's homemade double chocolate chip cookies in hand, she joined him at the round glass table. She still questioned her sanity for buying a glass dining table with so many children coming and going, but other than the persistent presence of small fingerprints, the glass had held up well so far.

Nate reached for a cookie, bit, chewed. "Wow. Powerful."

"I hope that means good. I tend to be a little heavy-handed on the chocolate, especially during high-stress days."

"With all these little ones underfoot, those are probably pretty frequent." He sipped at his milk, managing not to create a milk mustache. "What is this anyway? A day care?"

Rainy broke an edge off a moist cookie and held it between thumb and finger. "I'm a foster mom."

"They let singles do that?"

"The Department of Human Services is desperate for foster moms. So, yes. They do."

"That explains it, then."

She laughed. "Explains what? The total chaos?"

He had the grace to look guilty. "Well…"

"Today is unusual. You see, I normally take on only school-age children because I'm a teacher. I have to work. But last night, actually early this morning, I got an emergency call from the social worker about the two babies."

"Does that happen often?"

"Most calls do come at night, unfortunately. Nighttime seems to be when families fall apart. Drugs, drinking, and in this case, those eighteen-month-old twins were found alone in a car outside a casino."

She didn't mention the ongoing problem faced by the beleaguered social worker. There were not enough foster homes to care for all the needy children. And Rainy had trouble saying no, regardless of how full her house might be.

"The babies were in the car? While their mother was in the casino?"

"Yes. She'd been there for hours."

His horrified look matched her own reaction. "It's still cold outside."

March might be springtime, but at night the Oklahoma temperature tumbled to freezing.

"I know. Very cold, not to mention dangerous as all get out. Anyone could have stolen those children." She popped the bite of cookie into her mouth and almost sighed at the rich, gooey chocolate flavor. "That's why I agreed to take them until the social worker can find another placement, hopefully today."

"Brutal."

He could say that again. Foster care was not for the faint of heart. She'd heard some hair-raising tales and encountered far too many broken children, the exact reason she persevered. God had planted a mission inside her to make a difference in these forgotten kids' lives. And with God's help, she was succeeding, one child at a time.

"Another cookie?" She pushed the plate toward him. "Or will your wife be upset if you spoil your lunch with sweets?"

She hoped the question was as subtle as she wanted it to be.

As he chewed, Nate shook his head from side to side. "Nope. No problem there."

Okay, so she wanted to know for sure. Still playing innocent, she asked, "She doesn't mind?"

"She doesn't exist."

It took Rainy two beats to comprehend.

Nate Del Rio with the killer dimples was single.

Chapter Two

If there was one thing Rainy never wanted to be, it was a desperate, husband-hunting woman. So she refused to be happy that the handsome cowboy sitting across from her was unmarried. He was what he was. And so was she.

After she'd hung out her shingle to be a foster mother, with the intention of adopting as many kids as the Lord saw fit, she'd put aside her dreams of a husband. Mostly. If God dropped the right guy into her lap, she wouldn't argue. She just wasn't going out looking anymore.

"So how long have you attended Bible Fellowship?" Nate was asking.

"Since I moved here five years ago. It's a great church, lots of outreach to the needy, which I think is paramount, plus I love the small-group Bible studies. And the kids' ministry, of course."

"Of course." One side of his mouth quirked. "So you're not from around here, then?"

"Tulsa."

Both eyebrows joined the quirked lips. "City girl."

"I am not!" She leaned back in her chair, saw he was teasing, and laughed. "Well, not entirely. I like the smaller town life. That's why I took the job at Robert E. Lee."

"Summervale isn't too small anymore."

"No, but a good mix of small town and big city, don't you think?"

"Mostly. Traffic's gotten snarly since they put in the mall."

"Nothing like Tulsa at rush hour."

He shuddered. "Spare me that. Three cars on a country road are enough for me. What grade you teach?"

"Second. Five years, and I can't imagine doing anything else. Kids that age are a hoot—their wiggles, their gap-toothed smiles, their concrete, literal way of looking at the world."

He glanced toward the living room, where the children had adjourned. Mercifully, the house had settled into a quieter rhythm with only a now lower rumble of Cartoon Network and an occasional *shh* or giggle from one of the foursome.

"You like kids." His statement sounded a lot like an accusation.

"Crazy about them." Feeling no need to justify what was as natural as breathing, Rainy took another sip of milk. "What do you do, besides rush to the rescue of stressed-out women and their washing machines?"

"Ranch."

"Really? A real ranch, like with horses and cows?"

"You *are* a city girl."

"Am not," she said mildly. "So *do* you?"

"Have horses and cows? Sure. Mostly cattle since that's how I make my living. Angus beef. But I keep a few horses for fun. I mostly use a Mule for the real work these days."

Rainy leaned an elbow on the table, fascinated. She had no idea cowboys rode mules now instead of horses. The idea of lanky Nate on the back of a stubborn mule conjured up a funny mental picture, but she refused to laugh. The guy had gone above and beyond.

Besides, what she knew about ranches and cowboys would fit on a pencil eraser. But a ranch had animals. She knew that for certain, and animals were good for kids. She'd read any number of articles about their therapeutic value with people who were hurting. Like a tiny seedpod, an idea began to germinate.

She was always on the lookout for opportunities for the children, especially her boys. They needed far more than she could teach them. The only animal she had room or time for was Ralph, the fighting beta fish that only serious Will seemed the least bit interested in. But that was because Will worried about everything and everyone, considering himself the caretaker of the world.

A ranch meant lots of animals, lots of opportunities, maybe even healing of some of the hurts these children had experienced, and of equal importance, a male role model and a little recreation.

"Would you consider letting me bring the kids out to your ranch sometime?"

Nate blinked and the air around him stilled. "Why?"

What an odd question. "To see the animals, to see what you do on a ranch. Broaden their horizons. You know, the kind of experiences they won't get here in this crowded subdivision."

She loved her home and neighborhood with its family-oriented residents and tidy, colorful flowerbeds and walkways, but most of the yards were small, and houses butted up against each other on either side. A ranch meant room to spread out and run and be noisy.

Nate didn't appear to be of the same train of thought. Reluctance hung on him like a wet shirt. He studied the rim of his milk glass, gnawed one corner of his lip and didn't look at her. "A working ranch is no place for kids."

Weak excuse. And she was a teacher. Did he think she'd let him get by with that?

"Then, how does one learn to be a rancher?"

The question seemed to agitate him. He leaned forward, forearms on the table's edge, hazel eyes clouding toward mud-brown. "I grew up in the country. Farm animals were a part of the natural order of things."

Having taken to heart Christ's command to care for the needy and orphaned, Rainy was accustomed to pushing when it came to getting things for foster children. After all, she was on a mission for God. If God approved, she didn't care in the least if people found her pushy. "Are you implying that only those who grow up in the country can be farmers or ranchers?"

"That's not what I meant."

She smiled, feeling victory coming on. One more little push and he'd tumble like stacked dominos. "I'm so glad. I was positive a man thoughtful enough to join the Handyman Ministry would understand how much this could mean to at-risk town kids."

So it was a cheap shot. Rainy had no remorse.

Nate leaned back in his chair, hands dropping into his lap as he stared at her with exasperation. "You don't give up, do you?"

A tiny smile tickled Rainy's lips. "Never. Not when it comes to my foster kids."

This time, she was the one who leaned forward, pressing, determined as a terrier, her voice dropping low so the children didn't hear. "You met my kids, Nate, but you have no idea what they've lived through. They're survivors, but they carry scars. Will is too serious and considers the other children his responsibility. Joshua is my encourager, but he shivers and shakes at the first sign of conflict. Emma's charm can be manipulative. And Katie, poor little Katie—" She choked, tears filling her throat. She had not intended to go this far.

The cowboy across from her raised both hands in surrender. "Okay. They can come."

Rainy pressed back against the hard, wooden chair and drew in a deep, relaxing breath. Thoughts of what these children had suffered and witnessed always tore her apart.

"Sorry. I didn't mean to get teary on you."

"No big deal."

But she could see it was. Her handyman was ready to cut and run like a wild horse. Better grab the opportunity while it was knocking. Besides, one trip to the ranch would be a nice start, but she really had something more in mind. "How about tomorrow after church?"

He flinched. "So soon?"

"The weather is supposed to be decent tomorrow. And the kids will go wild with excitement. I promise to keep a tight rein on them. They're good kids." When he lifted a doubtful brow, she rushed on, "Really. I promise. Great kids. What do you say?"

Before he could answer, Katie's scream ripped through the air. Rainy pushed back from the table to see what was amiss this time.

"Great kids, huh?" Nate said without a bit of humor. "You could sell that scream to Hollywood."

Rainy chuckled anyway. "I know. Pure, high and blood-curdling. And most of the time, she's screaming about nothing." The scream, however, was Katie's way to communicate. "Katie has some issues we're working through, but today the scream might indicate another episode of throwing up. I'll have to check."

Nate got that helpless, eager-to-escape expression again. Well, who could blame the poor guy? No one—not even Rainy—liked dealing with a stomach virus.

As she pushed out of the chair, Will came into the kitchen. "Katie's all right. She's mad because I gave one of the babies a stuffed animal."

"No throw up?" she asked.

"No." The boy's serious eyes glanced at the cookies.

"Want one?" Nate offered the plate and then thought to ask Rainy, "Is it okay if he has one? He helped me out back there with the hose. Good worker."

Will took the cookie before she could reply, although she would have said yes anyway. "Joshy and Emma got scared. They're hiding in the closet again."

"Why?"

"Because there's a cop coming up the sidewalk."

Nate watched as Rainy Jernagen's face alternately paled and then flushed, a hot-pink color flaring on delicate cheekbones.

"Are we in trouble?" Will asked, his face alive with worry.

Rainy placed a hand on the boy's narrow shoulder, and in a soft, calm voice asked, "Have we done anything to be in trouble?"

"No, ma'am."

"Then we have nothing to fear from the police." She dipped her head low, making eye contact. "They're our friends, remember?"

From the way the boy's eyes shifted away, Nate figured he didn't buy that. Negative experience must have left a scar.

"Anything I can do to help?" he heard himself asking, though in reality, he'd had about all of the Jernagen house he wanted for one day. He was baffled as to why he wasn't escaping out through the garage.

On second thought, the police wouldn't look kindly on a male slithering out the back way while they stood on the front porch.

Rainy lifted blue-gray eyes to his, and he knew why he hadn't already cut and run.

A few minutes ago, she'd gotten to him with the mere hint of tears—he was a sucker for a woman's tears, as his sister well knew. And Rainy was kind and gentle and patient with the children, even though she was obviously running on adrenaline and little sleep. She was cute, too, now that her hair was brushed and she didn't look like a troll doll about to explode with stress. If he was truthful, she'd been cute all along, though he'd not wanted to notice.

But he was a man, and admiring a pretty, sweet woman came naturally. He couldn't change biology.

If she didn't have this passel of kids, he might even have asked her out.

A chill tingled his nerve endings.

If was a big, big word. He and kids didn't mix, and Rainy's devotion to the children was obviously more than a do-good activity to make herself feel charitable. She was passionate, with a missionary zeal.

Nate Del Rio simply did not understand the sentiment. Kids were a pain. Trouble. He knew from ugly, tenacious experience.

The doorbell played another round of hideous rock music. Rainy jumped.

She gave Will a reassuring pat on the shoulder and a gentle push. "If you'll check on Emma and Josh, I'll talk to the policeman first and then I'll be right in. Don't worry. Everything is fine."

She started into the living room, knees trembling. The nervous reaction made her almost as angry as the notion of someone intentionally frightening her kids. And she had no doubt this was the case.

Strong fingers caught her by the arm. "Why don't I answer the door?" Nate said. "So you can take care of the little ones."

She blinked her surprise, touched by his concern. "Thanks, but we've done this before. It will only take a minute."

He dropped his hold. "The police come here often?"

"More often than I'd like," she said grimly.

Kathy Underkircher and her hostility were wearing thin, for Rainy was certain that the woman who had decided to hate her for reasons that had nothing to do with these children had once again called the police.

"Why? You don't seem the kind to cause trouble."

"I'm not." She waved him off. "It's too complicated to explain right now."

The doorbell screamed again and, under other circumstances, Nate's flinch would have made Rainy laugh. The awful music had that effect on everyone.

"What is with the musical doorbell?" he asked.

"My brother installed it. His idea of a joke." She pushed a stray lock of hair behind one ear and said a little prayer as she gazed around the living room. The place looked better, if not perfect. But who expected perfect with children?

"Not your kind of music?"

"What?" she asked. "Oh, the bell. Despise it. Don't know how to dismantle it." She reached for the doorknob as the raucous tune restarted. Through gritted teeth, she said, "If that thing wakes the babies, I'll take a hammer to it."

Behind her Nate chuckled. "Sounds like a handyman job to me."

It occurred to her then that he was still here. By now the handsome cowboy—the handsome *single* cowboy—would be convinced he'd fallen into some alternative dimension filled with screaming kids, throw up, overflowing washers, irritating music and a policeman on the doorstep. Could her day get any worse? Might as well find out.

She ripped the door open with a little more force than needed.

A familiar officer in a blue uniform stood in the cool shade of the tulip-bordered porch. Sun glinted off his silver Summervale police badge.

"Miss Jernagen?"

"Hello, Officer Wagner," she said with a sigh. "Kathy Underkircher again?"

The policeman's head dipped slightly. "Anonymous caller. Sorry to disturb you but screaming was reported again. Is there a problem?"

The anonymous caller was Kathy, all right. The woman would never forgive her, no matter how she tried to mend the rift.

"None that needs police," Nate said, stepping up beside Rainy to extend his hand to the officer. "Nate Del Rio. Rainy and I attend the same church. Don't I know you?"

"Del Rio?" the young officer rubbed his chin. "Yeah, yeah. You got that ranch outside of town. Right?"

"That's right. Crossroads Ranch."

"My dad bought a heifer off you a while back for my little brother's agriculture project at school. I came with him to pick her up."

Nate's head bobbed. "I remember. Good breeding stock."

Rainy looked back and forth between the two men. It was considerate of Nate to be cordial but he had no idea she and Officer Wagner were old hands at this. She didn't need anyone to soften up the policeman with chitchat.

"Listen, gentlemen, I have four frightened children in there to attend to. Could we have this little reunion later?"

Chagrined, the officer nodded. "Sorry, ma'am. Do you mind if I come in? Check things out?"

"You know there's nothing wrong in here," she said.

"Yes, ma'am, but I have to check."

"I know. I know." She rolled her eyes heavenward, as much to beseech the Lord's help as for effect. "What a crying shame that Kathy can't get a life of her own and leave mine alone."

To let the officer in, she stepped back…and collided with

the cowboy. Strong fingers caught her upper shoulders. "Whoa now."

A few minutes ago, she'd been entertaining the idea of getting to know him better. Now that she was completely humiliated, she wanted him gone before she and her family further debased themselves in his presence.

"Nate, I appreciate your help in fixing the washer. Thanks so much. I'll call you later about visiting the ranch."

Nate didn't seem the least bit moved by her obvious dismissal. "Someone's crying back there."

Her head swung toward the back of the house and then returned to the officer. "I need to see about the kids."

"This will only take a minute."

"I'll go." Before she could protest, Nate's lanky legs carried him down the hall.

Surprised and more than a little touched, Rainy lifted both hands toward the officer and said, "Come on in and have a look. This morning has been incredibly hectic but all the noise is harmless, as always. Katie had a stomach virus. She screams when she hurts. Or about any other time she wants to communicate."

"Yes, ma'am. I understand." The officer glanced around the now tidy living room. "I see you have a couple of new ones over there."

"Temporaries. They arrived last night." She cast a glance toward the bedrooms. The crying had stopped.

Astonishingly, the twins remained asleep. As if he couldn't resist, the sturdy young cop headed toward the playpen. "I got one about this size. They can be into everything."

"These two have been so exhausted, they've mostly slept and eaten."

"That's not natural," he said with a chuckle. "Just wait till they get rested up."

"Hopefully, social services will find another placement for them by then. I'm not exactly set up for infants." She turned toward the hallway. "The other children are back here. But please be very gentle with them. They're terrified of you."

"I'm sorry about that, but I have to do my job."

"I know. Come on. Let's get this over with."

Officer Wagner was young, fresh-faced and genuinely kind, but that had never mattered to the kids. He wore a uniform and that was enough to set Joshua and Emma back for a week. Didn't Kathy Underkircher understand that the real victims of her animosity were innocent children? Even if she knew, would she care?

Bitterness gathered like acid on Rainy's tongue. She'd prayed about the woman, asking the Lord to deal with Kathy's hard heart. And now this. Again. On the worst day possible. In front of Nate.

Thanks a lot, Lord.

Whipping around, she led Officer Wagner through the house and pushed open the door to her bedroom. Her embarrassment at having two men see her unmade bed and pink pajamas was quickly forgotten. Nate Del Rio perched on the edge of her desk chair with Emma clinging to his knee like a blond wood tick. The boys were huddled next to his sides like baby chicks against a hen. In ordinary circumstances, the comparison of the hunky cowboy with a hen would have been amusing. Today, the sight was endearing.

"Everything okay in here?" she asked, her gaze searching each of the children's faces.

Will nodded solemnly. Joshua, bless his heart, trembled like an earthquake but followed his brother's example. Rainy's heart ached for the little guy. Emma's wide, troubled eyes were glued to the policeman.

"As you can see, Officer," Nate said, dropping a hand onto each of the boys' shoulders, "the kids are fine."

"Is this all of them?"

Katie chose that moment to answer for herself. She screamed.

Chapter Three

Nate didn't sleep a wink that night. Every time he closed his eyes, he saw Rainy Jernagen and her big-eyed foster kids. Worse, he felt the pressing weight of responsibility, worrying about them. None of which made any sense, other than he'd agreed to the foolish request to let Rainy bring the children to the ranch today. What had he been thinking?

Kids made him nervous. Not that he didn't like them, but he sure didn't want them running around the ranch getting into danger. Town kids wouldn't know the first thing about staying safe on a ranch. He'd known the dangers and still hadn't been able to avoid a tragedy.

The memory slapped him a good one, and following hot on its heels was the other memory. The one that kept him humble and praying for forgiveness.

He stalked through the kitchen toward the bubbling silver coffeemaker. His grandpa sat at the worn wooden table, glasses on the end of his nose, sipping stout black coffee and reading the Bible. As always, the sight touched a place deep inside Nate. Ernie Del Rio had come to the Lord after the tragedy that had nearly broken their family, and Grandpop's witness had eventually led his oldest grandson to Christ.

Nate would be forever grateful to his grandfather for loving him enough to lead the way. Sadly, neither his brother nor his sister displayed the least bit of interest in changing their ways.

As Nate's boots tapped across the tile, Grandpop peered at him over the top of his half-rims. "Looking rough, boy. You going to church?"

"Lousy night."

The old man poked a thick finger onto the printed page. "Says right here that the Lord gives His beloved sleep."

"Guess I'm not His beloved then." The truth was he'd long suspected he was low on God's list of favorites. But he understood and didn't hold it against the Lord. He had a lot to make up before God could be pleased with him, but he was working at it.

He dumped two spoons of sugar into his coffee, sipped and grimaced. "Pop, you make the worst coffee on earth."

His grandfather didn't take the grumbling to heart. "Don't drink it then."

They'd had this conversation at least once a week since Pop moved in with him three years ago. Grandma's passing had left the older man at a loss, and Nate needed help on the ranch. They'd blended their lives amicably—two old bachelors set in their ways, raising cows.

"Janine called a bit ago. I wrote the number on the pad."

"What now?" His sister was like a leech, sucking the blood out of him, always needy. He was the go-to man in the family, the only functional member of a dysfunctional mess. At least, he considered himself functional. He had a steady job and a permanent home, which was more than he could say for Janine and Blake most of the time.

He reached for the phone number, but Pop's voice stopped him. "Sit down and drink your coffee first. You don't have to jump every time she hollers."

Nate dialed anyway. Pop didn't understand. No one did.

Every time one of his siblings called, he got this sick pull of dread and fear in the pit of his stomach. What if...

"Janine? What's wrong?" There was always something wrong. She didn't call otherwise. "I thought you and Sal worked everything out yesterday."

"We did, Nate. I promise. Sal's being good as gold."

Nate grimaced. Sal was a beer-guzzling lout who came and went at will, leaving Janine and their baby to fend for themselves.

"So what's up?"

"Well, you see." She paused and he heard a shaky influx of breath. "Now don't get mad, Nate."

Nate braced one hand against the kitchen cabinet and stared out the window over the sink. Fat black calves grazed on two hundred acres of quickly greening Bermuda grass. His cows, his grass, his hard work, soon to be bigger and better if all went well.

"Just tell me what you want, Janine."

The whining commenced. "See? You're already getting mad. I can't help that I'm the unluckiest person in the world. You just don't understand what it's like to be in my shoes. You've got it made out there on your ranch. You've always had it made."

Nate didn't remind her of what they both knew. He'd started this ranch on a loan and a prayer, working sixteen-hour days for a long time. Since then, he'd leased an adjacent eight hundred acres with an option to buy. If he could save enough money before the lease ran out, the land would be his and he'd finally feel solvent as a rancher. But that was a big if, and Janine's constant requests for money didn't help him save any extra.

"My car broke down, and Bailey's out of diapers and milk."

Trying to hold his temper, Nate stalked to the table for his now-cooled coffee, grimacing as he drained the cup.

"Nate?" His name trembled from her lips.

"I gave you money yesterday." The silence told him everything. He flashed a glance at Pop but got no help from that corner. "Sal bought booze with it, didn't he?"

"Don't get mad. We paid the rent like you said, but everyone deserves to have fun sometimes. We went out for a little while to celebrate getting back together. You aren't married. You don't have kids. You can't possibly understand how hard it is." His sister's whine grew persuasive. "Anyway, Sal promised to look for a job tomorrow. They're hiring over at Wilson's Manufacturing."

Right. If Sal sobered up. Nate ground his back teeth together. "How much do you need?"

Pop made a rude noise and shook his head. Nate turned back toward the window. How he dealt with his sister's problems was his business, whether his grandfather approved or not. Times like this he wished for a cordless phone and a little privacy.

"Not much," Janine was saying. "A few hundred until Sal gets his first check."

Considering Sal was not likely to get a job, much less a check, any funds Nate dumped in Janine's pocket were a gift. Extortion, really. She knew he worried about her.

"I'll put a check in the mail in the morning."

Pop slapped his Bible shut. Nate didn't bother to look at the older man, knowing he'd see a glower of disapproval.

"Nate, I need money today. Bailey's whimpering right now because she's wet and I don't have any diapers. She'll be bawling for a bottle soon. And tomorrow I need to take my car in to have it looked at. That takes money. I'll pay you back, I promise. Just bring it here to the apartment this afternoon. Okay? This is the last time, the very last time I'll ask. Okay? For me. Please. I promise."

If he had a nickel for every time she'd made those promises, he'd be a rich man. "Where's Sal?"

"Sleeping."

Nate's mouth twisted. Sleeping it off, more likely.

"You don't want me to walk to the store, do you?"

The question sliced through him like a machete.

Janine knew her brother's every weakness, including his guilt, and Nate resented the thunder out of her manipulation. He also knew he was about to drive fifty miles to once more rescue his sister.

No wonder he never wanted to be a father. He felt as if he'd been one most of his life.

A new thought edged to the front of his mind. He didn't really want Rainy Jernagen's passel of kids hanging around Crossroads Ranch, getting into things, taking chances. Even though he'd agreed to let her bring them out after church, he now had a great excuse to renege without looking like a jerk.

For once, he was almost glad his sister had called.

Rainy exited the sanctuary of Bible Fellowship, gazing around in hopes of spotting Nate Del Rio. After Katie's timely scream yesterday, the police officer had rushed into her room to find the little redhead sitting up on her knees on the bed, retching all over the bedspread. Both he and Nate had made hasty retreats shortly thereafter. She didn't blame them one bit.

This morning, everything had looked much better. Katie's illness had passed. The social worker had found a great place for the twin babies. Rainy had actually slept eight full hours last night and worship service had lifted her spirits to new heights.

She squinted up at the blue March sky, where wispy mare's tails swirled, reminding her of today's outing at Crossroads Ranch. The idea of seeing hunky Nate again was pretty uplifting, too.

She couldn't forget that sweet moment when he had rescued Emma and Joshua from the back of the closet. He didn't even know those kids or her, and yet he'd lured them out of their most secure hiding place, something that had, on occasion, taken her an hour to do. Before the policeman arrived, she'd had the notion that Nate didn't like children. Guess she'd rushed to judgment on that one.

Joshua tugged her hand. Though dressed simply like his brother in a clean Henley shirt, blue jeans and tennis shoes, he was a handsome little boy. "Are we going now, Rainy?"

"To see the cows?" Emma asked. All spiffed up in fluffy church dresses and black patent shoes with white lace socks, Emma and Katie were as pretty as spring flowers. They stood together, the redhead and the blond, holding hands. At six and seven, they were close enough in age to be both best friends and worst enemies.

"Home to change clothes and have lunch first." She gazed around again but didn't see Nate.

"Hey, Rainy, got a minute?" A slender man in a green shirt and gold tie bounded down the steps, his toothy smile sparkling in the sunlight.

"Always have time for a friend."

Guy Bartlett was the youth and children's pastor. Rainy worked with the young minister on any number of projects. He was a nice man in an antiseptic kind of way and had even expressed an interest in her at one time. But all she could feel for him was friendship, which was too bad, considering his love for children. And she'd told the Lord as much.

Guy tweaked Emma under the chin and winked at Katie as he spoke to Rainy. "I was wondering if you would do a puppet presentation next week in Children's Church."

"Love to," Rainy said. One of her favorite ways of relating to kids was through puppets. "I've been working up a new skit about forgiveness."

"It'll be great. Your stuff always is."

"Well, thanks. I try." Since Katie's arrival three months ago, she'd had less time to spend on her hobby, but puppeteering came naturally. She'd be ready.

She expected Guy to take his leave. Instead, he cleared his throat, glanced toward the parking lot where cars were already departing, and said, "I'd like to invite the five of you out for Sunday dinner today if you don't have other plans. To discuss the children's ministry, I mean."

Rainy started to refuse, but then scoffed at the thought running through her head. Guy had clearly stated he wanted to discuss the children's ministry, not start a relationship. Even if she didn't find his company scintillating, they were friends and coworkers for Christ. When had she gotten so full of herself?

"Later this afternoon we're headed out to the country to see Nate Del Rio's ranch," she said, "but we have to eat first anyway. Right, kids?"

While murmurs of excitement rippled from the kids, Guy said, "Del Rio? Do I know him?"

"He attends Bible Fellowship, too. Part of the Handyman Ministry. He came to my rescue yesterday when a washer hose broke. I wrangled a visit for the kids to see the cows and horses."

Guy smiled. "Never miss a chance, do you?"

Rainy smiled in return. Her friends knew about her complete dedication to foster care. "Nope. Not if I can help it."

Joshua tugged on Guy's elbow.

"Can we go to Golden Corral?" the boy asked, hopefully.

Will scowled at his brother. "Shut up, Joshua. Don't be asking for stuff."

Guy squeezed Will's shoulder. "Golden Corral, here we come. A buffet is the best place for growing boys like you and me to get our bellies full. Right, Will?"

The teasing brought a tentative smile from the slight-built Will. As one of the smallest boys in fifth grade, nothing could make him happier than to grow taller.

"My car's parked in the south lot," Guy said, motioning in that direction. "Want to ride with me to the restaurant and I'll drop you back here afterward?"

Rainy was about to refuse, but the boys were already racing across the grass toward Guy's vehicle.

By the time they'd battled the long line at the restaurant, finished their meal and returned to the church, mid afternoon had arrived. Rainy was glad she'd gone, though, because the dinner had settled her mind about Guy's interest. They really had talked only about the ministry and, of course, her foster children.

With the kids anxious to get out to the ranch, they'd rushed back to the house, changed clothes and departed in record time. Rainy thought about giving Nate a quick call but then changed her mind. They'd agreed upon three o'clock. As reluctant as he'd been about letting the kids come, she was taking no chances. She would simply go as planned.

With the kids glowing with excitement, she aimed her minivan toward Crossroads Ranch.

With a sense of relief, an agitated Nate turned his truck beneath the crossbars of Crossroads Ranch. After an afternoon of trying to counsel Janine and Sal and listening to a dozen excuses about why they couldn't get their lives together, home was a much needed refuge of peace. Now more than ever he was glad he'd had the foresight to leave a message on Rainy Jernagen's answering machine, telling her not to come to the ranch.

The thought had no more than formulated when he rounded the curve in the long driveway and saw a green minivan parked next to the fat cedar tree in his front yard. He frowned, not recognizing the vehicle. Oh, well, he wasn't a hermit. He liked company. One of his buddies must have traded vehicles. All of them, it seemed, now had families. Everyone but him.

Finishing off the last slurp of a fountain drink, he parked his Crew Cab next to the green van and hopped out, expecting Yo-Yo, his border collie, to come flying around the house in ecstatic excitement.

The sun had disappeared, and clouds added a nip to the ever-present March wind. Still, the weather was pleasant and he considered taking the four-wheeler down to the fishing pond before dark. Bible Fellowship no longer had Sunday night service, urging its members, rather, to have family time.

He'd had all the family time he wanted for one day, thank you.

"Yo-Yo?" he called. No answer. Ah well, the dog must be outside somewhere with Pop.

As his boots thudded against the long, ranch-style porch, the sound of voices caught his attention. They came from back toward the barns and outbuildings, so Nate hopped over the end railing and rounded the house.

What he saw stopped him in his tracks. A groan escaped his throat.

Standing on the corral fence feeding carrots to the horses were four kids, his grandpa and Rainy Jernagen. Yo-Yo gazed on with pink-tongued adoration.

Nate looked heavenward, wondered if God was laughing at him or punishing him, and then stalked toward the giggling, wiggling, chattering group.

Backs turned, they didn't notice his approach. He planted his boots, his hands on hips and growled, "I guess you didn't get my message."

Six heads swiveled his direction. Yo-Yo leaped to his feet. Nate's scowl must have startled everyone except Pop, because he was the only one who spoke. Lowering his foot from the fence rail, his grandpop said, "Nate, boy, you made it back."

Obviously. "What's going on out here?"

"Rainy brought the children for a tour. Said you invited them."

No use explaining to Pop that Rainy had twisted his arm until he'd yelled "uncle."

"She told me what you done to help her yesterday," Pop said. "When the young ones got scared. Mighty nice of you."

Nate recalled squatting in front of a dark closet, assuring a shaking boy and girl that he was big and he could protect them. It was a lie. He couldn't protect anyone, but they'd come crawling out anyway, trusting him, messing with his heart.

"I called," he said, turning his attention to the guilty party. "Didn't you get my message?"

Rainy hopped down from the fence, dusting her fingertips together in a feminine gesture that didn't accomplish a thing but sure looked cute. With her hair pulled back in a ponytail, she looked fresh and pretty in jeans, sneakers and a blue hoodie that matched her eyes.

"What message?" she asked, smiling at him despite his obvious irritation.

"I left a message on your machine. Told you not to come, because I wouldn't be here."

One of her slender shoulders hitched.

"Sorry. I didn't get any message." She didn't look sorry at all. Neither did the kids, who now huddled around her, eyes wide as they stared between Rainy and him.

"Don't matter anyway, Nate boy," Pop said. "I've had a fine time showing them around. I'd forgot how much I enjoy having kids running around the place." His grandpa winked at Rainy. "Even if they are greenhorns."

As if the two were old friends, Rainy made a face at Pop and then said, "Your ranch is really beautiful, Nate. And so big. Your granddad was kind enough to drive us over the fields in the hay truck."

"We seen baby cows, too," Joshua said. "They're real nice. I petted one right on the nose and he licked me."

The boy extended a hand as if the image of a calf's tongue would be there as evidence.

Emma lifted a foot toward him, nose wrinkling. The bottom of her light-up pink sneakers was filthy. "I stepped in some…stuff."

"But she's not mad," Joshua hurried to say. "Are you, Emmie? She liked it. We like everything about your ranch. Crossroads is a real good ranch. The best I ever saw."

Probably the only one he'd ever seen, but at the child's efforts to please, Nate softened. The deed was done. Rainy and the children had had their visit to the country and nothing terrible had happened. He should be thankful, he supposed, that Rainy had come while he was gone. Now he wouldn't have to dread the visit. It was done. Over. Never more to return.

"So, you've had a good time then?" he managed, feeling a little guilty for his original gruffness. In truth, his bad mood had less to do with Rainy than his own family. No use taking his troubles out on her.

Rainy's sweet-as-honey smile was his answer. "The best. A field trip of this kind is beneficial. They've loved it. Thank you so very much for allowing us to come. I can't even express how special the afternoon has been."

Rainy Jernagen was as nice as she was pretty. And he was a certified jerk.

He displayed his teeth, praying the action resembled a real smile.

"Great." His head bobbed. "Glad you enjoyed yourselves." *And when are you leaving?* If she kept staring at him with that sweet smile, he might start having crazy ideas about inviting her again.

And that was not about to happen. No way, Jose.

"So," Pop said, clapping his hands together. "Why don't we all adjourn to the kitchen? I got some banana bread in there somebody needs to eat. Maybe a glass of milk. Whatd'ya say, Will? Could you use a little sustenance?"

Will grinned but didn't say anything. The rest of the group chorused their approval, so Nate had little choice except to fall into step. Yo-Yo, the traitor, didn't even bother to say hello. He was too busy making a fool of himself over the children.

"Katie went all afternoon without screaming," Rainy said to him.

"Good thing. That Hollywood scream might cause a stampede."

Rainy stopped in mid-step, eyes wide. "Really?"

Her reaction tickled him. "No. Not really. You *are* a greenhorn."

"Am not," she said amicably, and Nate wanted to tease her again. He liked teasing her. Liked her gullible reaction. He looked ahead where four children pranced around his grandpa, yapping like pups. He was glad they were up there with Pop and Rainy was back here with him. And no, he wasn't going to examine that thought too closely.

"Bet you wouldn't know a stirrup from a saddle horn," he said, baiting her.

"Guess I'm going to find out, Mr. Smartie."

Something in the way she sparkled with energy gave him pause. "What do you mean?"

"Your grandpa invited us back next weekend."

Nate battled back a cry of protest and more than a little panic. He shot a look at his grandfather's flannel-clad back. "He did?"

"Sure did." Rainy tapped his arm with one finger. "To go horseback riding."

Like a punctured balloon, all the air seeped out of Nate.

Without upsetting everyone—including his grandfather, who would never let him hear the end of it—Nate couldn't refuse. He wasn't that much of a jerk.

Uneasiness crawled over his skin like an invisible spider.

Of all the dangerous ideas, Grandpop would have to come up with this one. Horseback riding. Small children on the backs of very large animals with minds of their own.

A recipe for disaster.

He sneaked a glance at Rainy Jernagen's upturned face. His belly dipped.

From the moment she'd opened that red front door looking like a combination of mother earth and the bride of Frankenstein, he'd known she was trouble.

He should have run while he had the chance.

Chapter Four

Nate faced Saturday afternoon with a mixture of dread and anticipation. Long before Rainy's minivan zoomed down his driveway, he worked the horses on a lunge line, rode every single one of them to get rid of any pent-up energy that might cause an issue with inexperienced riders and checked all the tack for wear. But any cowboy worth his boots knew there was only so much he could do to prepare. The rest was up to the riders and the horses.

He shut the door to the horse barn and leaned there a moment to whisper a prayer that none of the visitors would get hurt. A cool, meadow-scented breeze dried the sheen of sweat from his forehead.

"Quit your frettin', boy, and come on. They're here." Pop came around the end of the barn from the direction of the calving shed.

Spring was calving time, and they'd gathered the expectant heifers into the lot for close observation. The old cows did fine birthing on their own most times, but the first calving heifers sometimes required attention. This crop of calves in particular was important to his expansion plans. He'd spent a fat sum of money on artificial insemination from one of the premiere Angus bulls. Sale of the calf crop would go a long way toward the purchase of the Pierson land next to his.

"We have better things to do today than entertain visitors," he groused.

"You been saying that all week."

"But you haven't been listening."

"Nope. Sure haven't." Pop clapped him on the shoulder. "Little relaxation won't hurt you none. Don't tell me a good-looking feller like you hadn't noticed how pretty Miss Rainy Jernagen is."

Nate kept quiet. Anything he said at this point would be used against him. Of course, he'd noticed. That was the trouble. But he didn't want to be attracted to a woman whose entire life revolved around children.

"I like them," Pop said.

Still Nate remained silent. Pop had decided to befriend Rainy and her pack of foster kids and nothing would stop him.

"Place needs a little noise. Even old Yo-Yo is tickled." Sure enough, Yo-Yo had dashed away, furry tail in high gear, at the approach of a car engine.

"They're your company," Nate grumbled, refusing to be mollified. "Not mine."

"Then I'm a lucky man." Pop rubbed his weathered hands together. "Here they come."

Sure enough, like a mama duck Rainy led her charges across the wide front yard. As soon as the kids spotted him and Pop they broke into a run, leaving Rainy to saunter alone.

Nate tried to remain focused on the children instead of Rainy, but somehow his eyes had a mind of their own. They zoomed straight to her.

Pop was right. She was pretty in a simple, wholesome manner. Not knock-your-hat-in-the-dirt, tie-your-tongue-and-make-you-stupid gorgeous, but pretty in a way that made a man feel comfortable around her. Made him want to know her better. Made his belly lift in happy anticipation.

Today she reminded him of the daffodils sprouting up in the front yard, bright and pretty and happy in a yellow fleece shirt above a pair of snug old jeans and black boots. He did a double take at her footwear and grinned. Rolled-up pant legs brushed the tops of a pair of spikeheel, zippered dress boots that sported a ruffle of fur around the top. Girly. Real girly.

"What you wearing there, Slick?" he asked, moseying out to meet her. He leveled a penetrating gaze at her fancy high heels.

"You said to wear boots if we had them."

"Um-hum. Boots." He angled one of his rugged brown Justin Ropers in her direction. They'd seen better days. "Real boots."

"These *are* real boots."

"Yep, if you're walking down Fifth Avenue in New York." His grin widened. "Or Tulsa. City slicker."

The corners of her full lips tilted upward. "Are you making fun of my choice in stylish footwear?"

"Sure am." In actuality, he thought they were feminine and sassy even if they weren't the best boot for riding horses, but giving her a hard time was easier than a compliment.

She waggled a foot at him. "Laugh if you want, cowboy, but I already had them in the closet. After I shelled out money for four pairs of kid boots this week, I decided these would have to do."

Hands fisted on his hips, Nate tilted back, his mouth twitching in amusement. "You bought the kids new boots for this one day?"

Rainy rolled her eyes. "Of course not. Your granddad said we could come out as often as we'd like, so I thought the boots a sound investment."

Suddenly the joke was on him. "Pop said that?"

She grinned. "Why do I get the feeling you're trying to get rid of us?"

Because I am. But he didn't say that. He did, however, send a scowl toward his annoying, meddling grandfather. What was the matter with that old coot anyway? He knew Nate's feelings about kids. He also knew the reasons his grandson never planned to have a family. He had one. One messed-up, constantly-in-need family was all he could handle.

"Nate, Nate!" Emma, the blond bombshell, barreled at him as fast as a first grader's legs could run. She didn't slow down until she slammed into his kneecaps.

"Whoa now." Nate caught her little shoulders. Bright blue eyes the color of cornflowers batted up at him. She was a gorgeous little girl, already stealing hearts. Some daddy would have his hands full with this one.

His chest squeezed at the thought. Emma didn't have a loving daddy to protect her.

"I got pink boots. See?" The little charmer twisted her foot this way and that for his perusal.

"Nothing but pink would do for Princess Emma," Rainy said.

"They're gorgeous, darlin'," Nate said.

The child's smile was as bright as Rainy's sweatshirt. "Joshy's got red ones and Will gots brown. He told Rainy he wasn't having no sissy boots. Will wanted man boots like yours."

Nate chuckled and glanced toward the corral, where Will and Joshua had gone. Both boys had their hands sticking through the fence. His smile disappeared. "You boys watch out doing that. If the horse thinks you have something in your hand, he might bite."

Both children yanked their hands inside and turned stunned faces toward Nate.

"They didn't know, Nate," Rainy said softly.

"That's the trouble," he groused. "They don't know anything about a ranch."

His sharp tone brought a puzzled look. "I'll keep a close eye on them."

"See that you do." He started toward the barn, where Pop was hauling saddles and tack out into the corral. Rainy kept stride, rushing a little as her fancy-heeled boots poked perfectly round holes in the soft earth.

"Will you teach us how to saddle the horses?" Hands shoved into her back pockets, yellow shirt as bright as the sunshine overhead, Miss Rainy's face was alive with interest and enthusiasm. Was she always so…so…optimistic?

He slid her a sideways glance. "Why?"

"Learning new things is good for the kids."

Yeah, so they could hang out on his ranch and bug him.

"And it will be fun, too."

He made a huffing noise, but Rainy didn't get the message that he was in a bad mood. She chattered right on.

"Where's your donkey?"

Nate tilted his head in question. "All you'll find on this ranch are cows and horses."

"But you said…" She bit her bottom lip, looking confused.

"I said what? That we own a donkey?" He remembered no such conversation. Was she losing it?

"Last Saturday at my house. You said you had horses for fun but you rode a donkey…" She paused, a small furrow between her pale brown eyebrows. "…or maybe it was a mule, for the real work. Aren't a mule and a donkey the same thing?"

Nate couldn't help himself. He laughed. Once he started he couldn't stop. He looked at his grandfather and things got worse. Pop leaned on a fence post doubled over, one arm pressed against his belly and a fist against his mouth. His cheeks flared out, ruddy and misshapen below his shiny, balding head. All around his feet riding tack lay scattered, as if he'd dropped everything the minute he'd heard Rainy's comment. The strangled, chuffling sounds coming from his short, round body were a failed attempt to be polite.

Nate's sour attitude vanished faster than tortilla chips at a Mexican restaurant. Hands on his thighs, he bent forward, his whole body shaking with laughter.

Meanwhile, Rainy and her children stared in bewildered curiosity at the two chortling ranchers. Joshua and Will exchanged glances, each lifting his shoulders in a shrug.

When Nate could finally catch his breath, he took Rainy's arm. "Come here. I want to show you something."

Still chuckling, he led the way into a covered area at the side of the barn where all vehicles, tractors, mowers, etc. were parked.

"This," he said, grinning as he approached an ATV with a small pickup bed on the back and a sturdy four-wheeler front. "Is the only Mule you'll find on Crossroads Ranch."

Emblazed across the vehicle's front were the words *Kawasaki Mule.*

"Oh." A becoming shade of pink neoned from Rainy's pretty cheekbones. She touched three fingers to her lips, lifted blue-gray eyes to his and giggled. "Oops."

Her cute reaction got him started laughing again. She joined him, laughing until she grabbed her side and said, "Stop. You're making me hurt."

By now, they were surrounded by the rest of the gang.

"Can we ride it?" one of the kids asked, awed by the camouflage green machine. Both boys had crawled inside and were investigating.

"Maybe sometime," Nate said before he could think better of such a promise. "Not today. Today we ride horses. Come on. I'll show you where the rest of the tack is kept."

"Can we pick our own horse?" Joshua asked, pointing. "I like that brown one."

"Champ's a good pony. We'll saddle him up."

"I want the blue one," Emma said, pointing toward a blue roan Appaloosa mare who grazed quietly outside the fence.

"Hold on there. We're only saddling three horses today—Champ, Patches and Bud." They were the oldest and most gentle.

"But there are seven of us," Will protested. "Do we have to share?" He said the last word as though it tasted sour.

Nate nodded. "Today you learn inside the corral. Grandpop and I will stay on the ground and teach. Maybe another time we'll all trail ride on separate horses."

Another dumb comment on his part. If he kept talking, the Brady Bunch would be regulars around here.

The group looked a little despondent, but Nate wouldn't budge on the issue of today's ride. Not one of them knew anything about a horse. Before he'd take them outside the corral, they needed instruction.

Demonstrating the proper method of saddling a horse took a while. Except for Will, the kids were all too small to lift the saddles or tighten cinches on their own. With Pop's help, Nate let the kids think they'd done the work. Saddling was the easy part. It was the riding that worried him.

"Okay, kids, go stand on the fence until I call your name."

All four of the children broke into a run. Emma ran directly behind the horses. One of the animals startled and hopped forward. Katie screamed.

Nate thanked God on the spot that all of his horses were dead broke and unfazed by the racket. The fact that Bud had jumped was proof, though, that even the best trained animal could be unpredictable.

He handed a set of reins to Rainy and one to Pop, taking the last one for himself.

"Ever ridden a horse before?" he asked Rainy as they led the horses forward into the center of the lot.

"Well…"

Nate looked heavenward. "That's a no."

"We can learn," she said, all chipper-like.

"Um-hum. Tell you what, I'll use you to show the kids how this is done. Then Pop and I will lead you around until you get the hang of it."

Which he figured would never happen.

"Sounds good." She dusted her fingertips in that pretty way and approached the horse.

"Other side," Nate said, hiding a smile.

"Does a horse know right from left?"

Was she serious? One look at her dancing eyes and he knew she was joking. "Most horses are trained to the right. Hear that, kids? Always approach a horse from the right. Never walk behind a horse where he can't see you. It scares him. And since he's a lot bigger than you, he might accidentally hurt you, not because he's mad but because he's scared."

Rainy did as he instructed, going to the right side. As he helped her into the saddle, her sweet scent mingled with the more familiar smells of leather and warm horseflesh. Coconut. She smelled like coconut. Keeping one hand on the reins and the other on the back of the saddle, he stepped back. A man didn't go around noticing how good a lady smelled if he wasn't interested in her. Which he wasn't. He couldn't be.

"You okay up there?" he asked.

Leather squeaked and shifted as she adjusted her feet in the stirrups. "Great. This is awesome."

At her delighted expression, Nate's heart bumped and he had trouble looking away. "Be careful of those high heels."

Concern creased her brow. "Will they hurt the horse?"

Nate's nostrils flared with humor but he held in a laugh. "Champ doesn't care what kind of boots you wear. For all I know he might even prefer fancy, furry lady shoes." Actually,

Nate was growing rather fond of them. "But heels that thin and long could get stuck in a strap or hung up in the stirrups."

"Am I in danger?"

"You're okay. I've got you covered." He hoped it was true.

The kids set up a howl. "When's our turn? I want to ride."

Nate shook off his unwanted entrancement with the lady and refocused on the children. There were four of them, all too young and inexperienced to go unsupervised for even a minute. Hadn't past experiences taught him anything about the dangers of kids and ranches?

"Hold on now. Miss Rainy and I are going to show you a few things first."

He ran through the basics, emphasizing safety for both horse and rider. No matter how hard he tried to concentrate on the kids, he was abnormally conscious of Rainy watching him from her horseback perch. He couldn't help wondering what she was thinking as she looked down. Was she watching to learn or because she liked what she saw?

The second notion made him uncomfortable, though he couldn't pinpoint the reasons. Maybe he should have shaved this morning.

Finally, Rainy said, "I think I can do this, Nate. And the kids are anxious to try. Let's give them a chance."

With a degree of anxiety, Nate helped her down and then queried each of the children on the lesson he'd just presented. Satisfied that none of them would do anything crazy, he assigned horses, and the adults each helped a child mount. Nate took responsibility for the little girls, putting them both on Patches, an old mare with the patience of Job. Rainy took Will, the oldest and most responsible, while Pop worked with Joshua.

After a while, the boys were riding on their own around the lot, blissfully unaware that the horses knew what to do without any help from the inexperienced riders. Pop walked along beside the boys, talking and instructing as they rode. With Will plodding around in a circle, Rainy drifted over to help Nate with the girls. At least that's what Nate told himself she was doing.

"Want me to saddle another horse for you?" Nate asked. "You look kind of bored."

Rainy, her hands inside the pouch of her daffodil sweatshirt, shook her head. "Not bored at all. Next time, though, I hope we can all ride together."

Oh yeah, next time. Uh-uh. "Maybe."

"The kids are doing really well, aren't they?" Her gaze slid to the two proud boys, sitting straight and tall in the saddle, listening to Pop as if their lives depended on it. Which, in fact, they might.

Grudgingly, he had to admit the afternoon had gone better than he'd anticipated. At least no one had been trampled underfoot or thrown over a fence. "Not bad for a bunch of tenderfoots."

"So you'll let us come back again?"

Did he have any choice? "I thought Pop already invited you."

"He did, but this is your ranch. I'd like to know you're okay with our visits, too."

Nate twitched under her scrutiny. She was smart. She knew he didn't want them here. She just didn't know why. And Nate was not about to share that little tidbit of guilt. "Why does my opinion matter?"

Rainy studied him with cool appraisal but changed subjects so quickly Nate couldn't help wondering. "Your grandfather told me you have a brother and sister. Do they live nearby?"

"My brother's in OKC." Or he had been last time Nate had bailed him out of trouble. "My sister lives on the other side of Tulsa. Why?"

"Just curious." She walked along beside him, her boot heels making *phht-phht* sounds as they sucked in and out of the loosely packed soil. "I only have one much younger brother. I envy people with big families."

She didn't know how lucky she was. Tempted to say so, he instead stopped the horse and spoke to the two little girls. "Ready to get off for a while, ladies?"

Two heads nodded, so he lifted Emma from the saddle first. She wound her arms around his neck and surprised him with a hug. "Thank you for the ride. I like your horse."

"Mighty welcome, Princess Emma." He handed the little girl off to Rainy, but her needy embrace lingered in his mind right next to Rainy's sweet coconut fragrance. "Come on, Miss Katie. Down you come."

He swung her up and out, braced for a scream that never came. Instead, she too hugged his neck. Nate swallowed a lump of disquiet.

"Can I lead Patches into the barn?" Katie asked.

"No, I want to," Emma said. Inserting herself between Nate and Katie, she worked those baby blues to good advantage.

"Girls, stop." Rainy went to her haunches in front of the children. "If you fuss, Nate won't want us to come back. Fussing scares the horses."

"Both of you can lead Patches," Nate said, handing a rein to each child, while keeping his hand on Patches' headpiece. The old mare would take herself into the barn, for that matter.

"You're certainly diplomatic," Rainy said, a smile in her voice as she fell into step beside him. "Ever consider a career in politics?"

Him? Diplomatic? Now that was a good one. "Ever consider a career in stand-up comedy?"

She laughed. "Maybe. I put on puppet shows. They can be funny sometimes."

One corner of the barn filled with hay caught the attention of Emma and Katie. They dropped Patches' reins and made a beeline for the bales, which were stacked in stair steps all the way to the open-beamed ceiling. Though prickly and itchy, Nate figured the hay was an otherwise great spot for the girls to play safely. He could keep an eye on them from about anywhere in the barn, and as long as he could see them, they'd couldn't get hurt or do anything dangerous.

He led Patches into a stall for unsaddling. Rainy trailed him, looping both arms backward along the top of the half-stall behind her.

"Seriously," Nate asked. "You do puppet shows?"

"Don't look so stunned, cowboy. Even a city slicker has hobbies." She looked around the boxy, cell-like structure. "Can I help in some way?"

The confines were crowded with the three of them inside, though the wide-rumped mare took up much of the space. Smells of dusty hay and sweaty horse mingled with well-worked leather and sweet coconut. That coconut was going to kill him before the day was over. He was sure of it.

"Grab a brush over there." He motioned toward a wall, where various types of grooming tools hung from hooks. "You can brush her mane. She likes that." He pulled hard on the cinch buckle, loosening the tight belt around the horse's middle. "Got a horse puppet?"

"Might get one now that I'm an expert cowgirl." She came up next to him, brush in hand.

Nate decided he liked her gentle humor, liked teasing her and knowing she would appreciate the effort.

"Well, Slick, being how you're an expert and all, why don't you remove this saddle and brush Patches down?" He stepped back, grinning.

The cute greenhorn took the comment as a challenge.

"You think I can't?" She made a proud little sniffing

sound, tossed her head, and then bumped him with one shoulder. "Move over, Cowboy. Let me show you how it's done."

Feeling unusually lighthearted, Nate stepped back and crossed his arms over his chest. "She's all yours."

"Okay, I can do this." Rainy bent low to look under Patches's belly. "All unhooked. Okay. That's a start." She patted Patches's neck and leaned close to the mare's ear. "If it's all right with you, Patches, I'm going to take this big old saddle off your back. You'll feel so much better when I do. Ready now?"

A snort escaped from Nate. Rainy shot a pretend glare in his direction. With slender arms that didn't look strong enough to lift a feather, she grabbed the saddle by the horn and the back and pulled.

"Easy now," Nate said, as much to Rainy as to the horse. He uncrossed his arms, ready to jump in with assistance.

The saddle came all at once, its weight bearing down unexpectedly. Rainy staggered. Nate reached in from behind and added his strength to hers. Together they levered the saddle onto the stall divider. He'd move it to the tack room later.

"I could have managed," Rainy said, her breath puffing softly from exertion as she turned toward him.

Still standing a little too close for comfort, Nate grinned down into eyes sparkling with fun. "I know you could have, Slick. First time's always the hardest."

He expected her to slither away from the close contact. Instead, she grinned back at him and stayed put. His pulse ratcheted up a notch.

When she and her pack of kids had come to the ranch today, he'd expected nothing but trouble. Instead, he had actually enjoyed himself. Nothing bad had happened. No one was injured by a frightened horse. And he hadn't minded getting to know Rainy better.

Maybe this wasn't so bad after all.

The idea drifted through his mind that he wouldn't mind kissing her, either. With one hand propped on the wall above her head, he thought how easily he could lean in and give it a try. Nothing wild and crazy, just a friendly kiss. An end to a pleasant day.

Before he could move, a distant rumbling penetrated his consciousness. And then a shout.

"What was that?" Rainy had barely spoken the words when Nate pivoted away.

Another shout and then the roar of a motor.

Ice cold fingers of fear gripped him. He broke out of the barn in a dead run in time to see Joshua bouncing across the barnyard on the Mule. Alone.

Nate almost went to his knees.

He'd let his guard down.

Now something terrible was about to happen. Again.

Chapter Five

Rainy's pulse thundered in her ears as she raced out into the sunlight. Her blood ran cold at the sight before her. Joshua, alone on the high-powered Mule, bounced out of control over the rough pasture. White as milk, his eyes bugged out and his thready voice rose in terror above the roaring motor.

"Miss Rainy! Miss Rainy!"

Rainy screamed back, "Push the brake," knowing full well Josh didn't know a brake from a gas pedal. In fact, from all appearances, the terrified child had frozen in fear, inadvertently holding the throttle wide open.

Nate, who'd exited the barn so fast she'd needed a minute to understand what was happening, now ran after the fleeing vehicle. His boots pounded hard and fast against the newly sprouted grass.

At the shouts, Nate's grandfather, accompanied by Will, came out of the tack room. The girls ran crying from the hay barn.

"Joshy, Joshy," Emma yelled. "Miss Rainy, Joshy's going to get hurt.

Her throat drier than chalk dust, Rainy feared Emma was right. There was no way Nate could stop the runaway vehicle.

"Dear God, please help." She said, "Pray, kids. Pray."

With growing fear and a terrible sense of helplessness, she watched the scene play out. As if in slow motion, the Mule headed toward a pond in the distance. With oversized tires and four-wheel drive, the machine bounced up and over terraces, in and out of holes, and wildly careened over jutting rocks and fallen tree limbs. In minutes, Joshua would hit the water…and even if he wasn't injured on impact, he couldn't swim.

Rainy's knees quaked. "Jesus, please. You put these kids in my safekeeping. I'm so sorry I let you down. Help. Please help."

A flurry of "should haves" ran through her head. She should have been watching him better. She should have known a curious boy might tamper with what he considered a fancy riding toy. She should have been out in the lot with him instead of inside the barn drooling over Nate's killer dimples.

Because of her carelessness, Nate was in danger, too. With growing fear, Rainy knew he had every intention of stopping the Mule, even if it meant sacrificing himself. As if he could, by brute strength, stop a fifteen-hundred-pound moving vehicle, he ran toward Joshua at an angle to cut him off.

The runaway machine barreled toward him at full tilt. Joshua held on, screaming. As Nate and the ATV crossed paths, the cowboy grabbed the side of the front grill. He shoved his boot heels into the ground. The overpowering machine wrenched him sideways like a rag doll. Nate's body flopped wildly. He held on, his muscles straining beneath sweat-drenched chambray.

Like a stunt man in an action movie, he threw himself over the hood and clung to the front roll bar. Slowly, slowly, he edged forward until, at last, he leaned inside and killed the switch.

The sudden silence pulsed across the green grass. Shaking so hard she needed to sit down, Rainy sagged with relief. She slid onto the ground and sat for a full minute, hugging Emma and Katie to her side.

"Thank you, Jesus," she whispered.

The Mule's motor kicked on again, this time with Nate at the controls. Still trembling, Rainy waited near the gate. As the ATV passed her, Rainy's heart sank. Judging by Nate's cold-as-January expression, they were in big trouble.

Along with the remaining children, who hovered around her like baby birds, she followed the Mule into the shady vehicle shed.

Nate killed the ATV and stepped out.

"How did this happen?" he demanded to no one in particular.

Rainy reached for the terrified Joshua, pulling him off the ATV and into her arms. When he fell against her and burst into tears, she dropped to her knees and held him close. Barn dust and a little boy's terrified sweat assailed her nostrils.

"I'm sorry, Miss Rainy, I'm sorry. Don't be mad." His body quaked as his tears drenched her neck.

Other than soothing noises, Rainy didn't know what to say or do. The anger radiating from Nate Del Rio was enough to make anyone cry. This was all her fault. Joshua was only a little boy. She should have been watching him instead of flirting with Nate.

The other three children hovered in the entrance, stunned to silence. From the looks of them, they all expected to be deported to Siberia on the next train.

Rainy's protective mama gene kicked in. Joshua had made a mistake, but she wasn't about to let Nate Del Rio or anyone else scare him any worse than he already was. "It's all right, kids. Don't be scared. Joshua isn't hurt."

Three pairs of eyes darted to Nate's grim face. His arms

crossed, the cowboy leaned against the fender of a red tractor, ominously quiet.

About that time, the elder Del Rio appeared from the other side of the tractor and headed straight for Joshua. "Now, boy, quit your crying. Nobody's mad at you. You scared us, that's all."

He gave the boy a reassuring thump on the back.

Rainy's focus moved from the children to Nate. Was his grandfather right? Was Nate frightened instead of angry? Over Joshua's trembling shoulder, she studied the ring of white around Nate's lips and the sheen of sweat on his forehead.

"Me and Will went in the tack room," the elder Del Rio said. "I figured Joshua would tag along. Figured wrong. Figure I'm the one who left the key under the seat, too. So if anyone's to blame here, I reckon it's me."

Some of Rainy's defensiveness fled. Ernie Del Rio was a kind man. Gently, she urged Joshua to his feet and swiped a sleeve over his teary face.

"Blame isn't what's important. What matters is that Joshua is safe and he's learned a lesson. Nate," she said, forcing her gaze up to his, "thank you for what you did. You may have saved Joshy's life."

Stiffly, Nate pushed off the tractor. With a shaky inhalation, he went to one knee beside her and the boy.

"Do you understand why we're upset, Joshua? The machines on this ranch are not toys. You can get seriously hurt pulling a stunt like that."

Joshua's brown head nodded, his body still trembling in a way that made Rainy want to shoo Nate away. But as a teacher, she knew Joshua should not be protected from the consequences of his actions. Otherwise, he'd do something foolish again. Next time the outcome might not be so positive.

"You need to apologize, Joshua." To ease her demand, Rainy stroked Joshua's back over and over again. "Tell Nate and Mr. Del Rio that you will never, ever do anything like this again."

The nine-year-old's reddened eyes filled. In a broken whisper, he said, "I won't."

Straightening his little spine, he stepped toward Nate to extend a trembling hand. His brown hair was sweat-stuck to a still pale forehead. "Thank you for saving my life. I won't make you have to do it again."

Rainy pressed her lips together to keep from smiling and crying at the same time.

"I believe you're a man of your word, Joshua," Nate said, taking the small offered hand into his much larger one.

The fact that Nate used his left hand and kept the right one crooked against his belly caught Rainy's attention. She studied his slow, careful movements. In all the commotion, no one had considered that Nate's heroics could have caused him injury. Indeed, his right shoulder seemed to hang at an odd angle.

"Nate, are you hurt? Your arm—"

He shot her a silencing look. "No big deal."

"I think it is." She touched his shoulder. He winced.

"I said I'm fine, Rainy. Let it go."

She pulled back, stung by his sharp retort.

"All right, then," she said stiffly. "Guess it's time for us to head home. Come on, kids. Tell the gentlemen thank you."

An obedient, if somewhat subdued, chorus of voices rose and fell, and then all four kids decided a bathroom run was in order before departure.

Eager to escape the moody cowboy, Rainy waited just inside the back doorway for the children. In minutes, they all returned carrying cans of soda and prancing around Nate's legs, clamoring for his attention as if nothing had gone wrong today.

Even though his color remained pale and he cradled his arm against his chest, Nate had made the effort to encourage the kids. He'd given them a cola and brought a smile to their gloomy faces. She had to appreciate that.

Nate Del Rio was the most disconcerting male she'd met in a long time. One minute he was gruff and the next he did something incredibly heroic or kind. She didn't know whether to hug him or kick him in the shins with her pointy-toed boots.

"Thanks for today," she said to the elder Del Rio, who insisted she call him Pop like everyone else. "I'm sorry for the trouble."

Not that Joshua's mishap would keep her from bringing the children here again, but she really was sorry the incident had taken the gloss off an otherwise shining day.

Pop waved her off. "Ah, stuff happens. Don't fret, Rainy. Kids gotta learn. That's why you brought 'em out here."

"Thank you," she said, smiling into hazel eyes much like his grandson's. "For understanding."

Which was more than she could say for the other Del Rio. The one with the killer dimples.

Feet tired from standing in heels all afternoon, she tottered a bit as she started toward the van, where four youngsters jockeyed for favorite seats. She was painfully aware that Mr. Dimples was standing in the yard, watching her.

"Rainy."

She stopped, drew a fortifying breath and pivoted.

Nate blinked at her, his expression uncertain. Rainy's heart fluttered.

She softened. "What?"

He waited two beats, eyes raking her face. Then he shook his head, his dimples flashed and his voice went soft. "Drive carefully."

Rainy figured it out on the drive home. Nate wasn't angry or cranky or rude. He just didn't want her to worry about his injury.

"Too late, Mr. Del Rio," she muttered.

"Huh?" Will, in the front bucket seat, turned in question. "Did you say something, Miss Rainy?"

"Talking to myself, Will." She glanced in the rearview mirror at the other kids, quiet for the moment. Katie's red head lolled to one side, her eyes droopy. In fact, they all looked worn out, a good thing when riding in a car. She'd broken up more than her share of energetic quarrels when the ride lasted too long.

"I feel bad for what happened," Will said, his fingers fidgeting on a now empty soda can.

"I do, too, honey." Even worse to know Nate had been injured in the process. "We'll have to think of something nice to do for Nate and his grandfather."

"I could offer to help out on the ranch. Feed horses and cows, muck out the barn and stuff like that." He pushed at the nosepiece of his glasses. "If you'd look after Joshua and Emma for me, I mean."

"That's not your job anymore, Will."

"I know." He glanced out the side window, his profile serious.

From what she'd learned of the children's pasts, Will had been their primary caregiver since he was very small. If the little ones caused a problem or lacked anything, he was blamed and often punished when and if the mother came home. His overblown sense of sibling responsibility weighed heavily.

"This needs to be a team effort. Let's see if we can come up with something we all can do."

"Like what?"

"Well," she said as she tapped her fingers on the steering wheel, chagrined to see dirt under her nails, "we could bake them a cake or some other goodie. I've heard bachelors don't get many home-cooked foods."

"Brownies." Even though he didn't smile, the child's face lit up with interest. "And a puppet show. Everyone likes your puppet shows."

Including a certain boy who could use a little more childhood in his life.

"Will, my man, you are a genius. Brownies and a puppet show it is."

"I asked them to come again next Saturday."

"You didn't." Nate shoved aside the cow-calf ledger he was working on to glare at his interfering grandfather. Four bull calves born this week without a problem. The Lord was blessing his hard work. Finally. Now if he could get Pop off his back about Rainy Jernagen so he could stop thinking about her, life would be good. "After what happened, today was enough."

He reached for the glass at his elbow. A pale brown mix of melted ice and watery root beer condensed into a ring atop well-worn wood. Nate pushed back from the table to get a refill.

Pop beat him to it, taking the glass from his hand and going to the freezer. Ice rattled.

"No use getting your tail in a twitch. Poor little kids was so upset. I figure they need to come back so's they'd know we wasn't mad at 'em."

Nate raised his eyes heavenward. His arm ached like nobody's business and he had a headache from thinking of all the things that could have happened if he hadn't been able to stop the Mule in time. That cute little boy with the big blue eyes and gentle ways could be laying in a hospital—or a morgue.

A shudder ran through him. Some memories weighed too heavily. He couldn't take a chance on repeating a nightmare.

He stalked to the sink and stared out at fat black, peacefully grazing cattle. Usually, the sight soothed him, edged out the mental flashes of Christine. Not so today.

"It's too dangerous, Pop."

"Living is a dangerous proposition, Nate boy. The roof might cave in any minute. Or a stampede of buffaloes could tear through the wall and trample us both to death."

Nate's lips twitched. Turning, he leaned his hip on the brown granite countertop. "There isn't a buffalo within fifty miles of here."

Pop shoved a glass of root beer at him. "That's what I'm trying to tell you. No use borrowing trouble."

Shaking his head, Nate laughed. "You make me feel better, even if you don't make any sense."

"Now don't tell me you aren't interested in seeing that pretty little lady again. Cause if you do, I'll have to remind you that lying is a sin." He opened the refrigerator and peered inside. "What do you want for supper?"

"Anything." Nate sipped the syrupy sweet pop, welcomed the fizz as liquid cooled his throat. "Getting distracted by Rainy is what caused the problem in the first place."

Pop straightened up, one hand holding to the top of the refrigerator door. "So *that's* what's eating you. You're blaming yourself for Joshua's curiosity."

Root beer soured in Nate's stomach. The responsibility was his, plain and simple. "He could have been killed. On *my* ranch."

"Didn't happen." Pop jabbed a fat finger at him. "Cast down imaginations, boy. That's what the Word says."

Nate knew his granddad was right. He shouldn't worry. He shouldn't always expect the worst to happen to people he cared about.

The notion caught him up short. He'd spent minimal time with Rainy and her charges, but somehow they'd gotten under his skin. He didn't like them there, didn't want them intruding on his thoughts. He didn't need anyone else to worry about.

Because no matter how much he prayed, his past mistakes lingered behind his eyeballs as ghoulish reminders. He wasn't sure he could live through another tragedy. Especially if he was the cause.

Pop plopped cellophane packages of bologna and cheese onto the table. "Go on. Call her. Let her know you aren't mad."

Nate pulled bread from the cabinet, adding the loaf to the pile. Cold cuts worked for him. He was in no mood to cook.

"I wasn't mad. Did she think I was mad?"

"Yep." Grandpop reached around him to where the phone hung on the end of the cabinet, its curly cord wadded into a mess. He handed the receiver to Nate. "Go on."

Nate stared at the dial pad for several seconds and then returned the phone to the hook.

Some things were better left alone. Thinking he was angry might not be such a bad thing if the notion kept Rainy Jernagen and her sweet smile at arm's length.

Sunday afternoon Nate opened his front door and came eyeball to eyeball with Rainy's sweet smile in the form of a giant yellow happy face puppet. He was certain the human behind the puppet was Rainy because she was accompanied by four much shorter puppets. And he smelled coconut.

His belly dropped into his boots. So much for avoidance.

Smiley's huge mouth opened. "A little birdie told us—" she started.

Up popped a crow puppet. "Cheep, cheep, cheep." Emma's blond hair peeked out from either side. "Cheep, cheep, cheep."

"Enough cheeping, Emma," Will's voice whispered from behind a cross-eyed pig. "Let Rainy talk."

"I want to be sure Nate hears me," came Emma's stage-whispered reply. Mouth unmoving, the crow repeated, "Cheep, cheep, cheep."

Nate laughed in spite of himself.

Smiley cleared her throat. "A little bird told us that you did a very nice thing for someone. We came to say thank you."

"We brought brownies, too!" Joshua's face appeared from the side of a flop-eared dog.

Nate reached up and slowly pushed the yellow smiley downward until he was peering into Rainy's gray-blue eyes. "What is this, the Happy Patrol?"

The sweet smile he didn't want to think about appeared. "Something like that. Let us in and we'll entertain you with a skit."

No use fighting the inevitable. Rainy was a velvet bull-dozer, and she'd mow him down and probably make him enjoy the experience. "Did I hear brownies mentioned?"

"My own special recipe. With chocolate chips."

"Double chocolate, huh? Having a rough day?"

The smile widened and she waved the happy-faced puppet. "You can decide after you taste them."

"Deal." He motioned them inside, quickly scanning the living room. He needn't have worried. With only two people to pick up after, the house stayed neat and tidy, the way he liked things. Everything in its place, unlike the chaos he'd seen at Rainy's. "Pop's not here. This is his day to visit the nursing home."

Rainy's gaze traveled lightly around the open ranch-style room, over the dark wood and leather furniture, the fifty-inch plasma television, the sturdy walnut tables, and came to rest on the native rock fireplace. Considering he'd collected the rocks himself, he was especially proud of that fireplace.

"Do you have someone special in the nursing home? A relative, perhaps?"

"Souls," he said. Then, seeing her quizzical expression, he explained. "Pop was older when he came to know Jesus. He feels older folks are often overlooked."

"I guess that's true," she said softly. "What does he do there?"

"Whatever they ask. Writes letters, reads the Bible, prays. Mostly he listens."

"Your grandpa is what I'd call a real Christian."

Nate had to agree. He wished he could be more like Pop.

Without a peep, Rainy's tribe of four lined up on his sofa like soldiers for inspection. She must have warned them to be on their best behavior.

"Yeah, Pop's a good guy," he said, motioning Rainy into a seat next to the hearth. He took the chair opposite her.

"So is his grandson. How's your arm?" Rainy leaned toward him, the yellow puppet speaking for her. "Don't try to tell me you weren't injured. I know better. Smiley knows everything."

Nate rotated the shoulder for effect. "A little sore. Tell Smiley it's nothing permanent."

"I'm glad. Smiley and I are both glad, aren't we, Smiley?" The puppet turned to face her and nodded, its wide mouth flopping open and closed several times before Rainy laid the toy in her lap and said, "Seriously, Nate, what you did yesterday was amazing. Brownies and puppets are not enough to express how thankful I am."

What he'd done yesterday should never have happened, but he wasn't in the mood to go there. Rainy and her trouper of puppeteers cheered him. Why ruin a good mood? She was here and, short of throwing her out, she was likely to stay a while. He would avoid her next time.

"Brownies are a start," he said. "Are we going to eat 'em or admire 'em?" He lifted his eyebrows toward the container Joshua had placed on the coffee-table.

"We made those for you and Pop," Rainy said, "not for us."

"Ah, come on now. No fun eating brownies alone. I think that's a rule somewhere. Right, kids?"

Four sets of blue eyes shifted to Rainy and then back to the brownies. She laughed. "Little piggies. It's not as if you never get brownies."

Will raised his puppet.

"But, Miss Rainy," he said in an oinky pig voice, "you got to fatten us up. Skinny pigs don't win prizes at the fair."

Rainy's face glowed at Will's attempted humor. From what she'd told Nate, the boy didn't have much to laugh about most of the time.

"Will's right, Miss Smiley Face. I'm a rancher. I know these things."

"I can see I'm outnumbered." She eyed the fearsome foursome. "I have dinner in the crock pot at home, so only one for each of you this time. Okay?"

"And milk," Nate said with a conspiratorial wink at the children. "Can't have brownies without ice-cold milk."

A row of blue eyes danced, but no one except Nate moved. He looked from the kids to Rainy and back again. She must have read them the riot act. "They can get up, Rainy."

"They're really sorry about yesterday, Nate. They don't want to do anything to upset you. They absolutely love coming out here and have talked nonstop about nothing else since."

The comment hit him right in the heartstrings. They were little kids. Good kids. Pop was right. Children were naturally curious. They made mistakes. Maybe he'd been too gruff.

"Yesterday's over, kids. Understand? I've made my share of dumb mistakes. Learn from them and move on. Okay?" He only wished he could take his own advice. He waited two seconds while his words settled in and then pumped his eyebrows. "Last one in the kitchen is a rotten egg."

Four small bodies erupted from the couch. Nate braced himself for a brawl—or, worse yet, one of Katie's Hollywood screams.

"Now you've done it," Rainy said, following him and the wild bunch into the big country kitchen.

The young ones skidded to a stop on the rock tile and with a cacophony of laughter and excited voices, pointed at Rainy. "You're last. You're a rotten egg."

She raised her smiley puppet with one hand and the brownie container with the other. "But I have these. So what do you say? Am I still a rotten egg?"

Good-natured groans and mumbles and giggles rose from the children.

Nate trucked to the refrigerator for the milk, all the while observing the interplay between Rainy and her crew. A genuine affection flowed between them. His first impression of a harried woman with out-of-control kids had been way off. Rainy Jernagen not only had control in a firm, loving manner, she was…amazing.

Taking the milk carton from his hands, Rainy poured as he set a small glass in front of each child. He breathed a sigh of relief that Janine had left behind a complete set in one of her many comings and goings. Dishes weren't high on his shopping list. Certainly not kid-size dishes.

"Josh, grab us a paper towel over there, will you?" Nate nudged his chin toward the holder beside the sink. Will started to rise but sat down again, apparently realizing Joshua could handle the task. Solemnly, the younger boy placed a curling square of paper in front of each person. Katie was already peeling back the lid on the Tupperware container, her freckles popping with effort. Rainy lifted one finger in gentle reminder and passed the brownies from child to child.

Nate scraped a chair back from the table to join the party, the scent of baked chocolate tantalizing his senses.

"I didn't see you at church this morning," he said when she passed the Tupperware his way.

In truth, he'd done his best to avoid her, but that had required an inordinate amount of crowd searching and attentiveness to his surroundings. Then he'd spent the rest of the service asking the Lord's forgiveness for thinking about her too much instead of concentrating on worship. No wonder he wasn't priority one with God.

"Children's Church," she said, cupping a hand under her chin to catch any brownie crumbs. "I presented a new puppet show today."

"How'd it go?"

"Good, I think. The class laughed and interacted with Brian the Brain, my genius puppet who thinks he knows everything."

"Does he?"

He took his first brownie bite. The power of rich, gooey double chocolate almost made him moan. He'd never had anything quite like Rainy's special recipe.

"No, that's the fun of it. Brian's arrogant about his intellect, so when the kids catch him making silly mistakes—and I make sure they do—they love it. He's a great tool for teaching life lessons."

"Am I meeting Brian the Brain today?"

She shook her head. "Uh-uh. Brian stayed home. You've already met today's entertainers. Normally, I'm a one-woman show, but the kids wanted to do this special skit just for you—as a thank you, an apology." She lifted her shoulders. "Because they like you. So they're helping today."

A few brownie crumbs dropped onto her paper towel. Poking at them with her index finger, she leaned close to whisper, "Don't expect anything fancy."

Her face was close enough that Nate noticed the spray of thick brown lashes fanning the crests of her cheekbones. And caught a whiff of that maddening coconut. The light, airy feeling lifted higher, filling his chest with warmth.

He didn't want to be attracted to Rainy, but he was. If only she wasn't so committed to kids....

Swallowing, he glanced toward the foursome gathered around his square table. They chattered among themselves while savoring their snack. The two girls each wore a milk mustache. Joshua swiped a sleeve across his mouth, coming away with a streak of chocolate on his cuff. Will frowned at him and handed over his clean paper towel, urgently whispering something. Josh looked down, saw the chocolate and scrubbed at the spot.

Nice kids. But Janine and Blake had been good kids, too, at one time. Now look at them. Excellent examples of why he should not get sentimental about Rainy's foster children.

"Are you ready for our show?" Rainy was asking as she wadded her paper towel and glanced around for a trash can.

"Whenever you are." He took the paper from her. "I'll clean this up later."

Rainy paid him no mind. In seconds, she and the children cleared away the glasses and towels. Then they adjourned to the living room for the performance.

Amid much nervous giggling from the youngsters, Rainy parked Nate in a chair. Then she and the children took positions behind the sofa across from him. As the only audience, he suffered a moment of discomfort. What exactly did they expect from him?

Four puppets popped into sight above the back of the couch. So commenced a skit about a super dog in a cowboy hat and a red cape who saves a foolish pink pig from running in front of a truck. Throughout the performance, the four children alternately giggled and shushed and forgot their lines. Thumps of movement shook the sofa.

Filled with cute one-liners, the show was a thinly disguised reenactment of yesterday's incident. Nevertheless, Nate found himself alternately amused and touched by the message of friendship, apology and forgiveness.

So when the skit ended and the five puppeteers rose for a bow, Nate rose with them, applauding. From the children's flushed and thrilled expressions, he figured they'd had limited accolades in their lives. The notion stung.

In that moment, the old feelings of responsibility pressed in. If he could make a difference in their lives, shouldn't he be willing? Wouldn't God expect it?

Some of the pleasure from the puppet show seeped away. Sometimes God was a hard taskmaster.

Chapter Six

Rainy waited until the social worker pulled out of the drive before she closed the door. With a sigh, she leaned against the hard wood and smiled at a skinny, freckled, frightened eight-year-old boy named Mikie. The social worker had come for a scheduled visit to discuss Rainy's desire to adopt Katie. Katie, as usual, had screamed bloody murder the minute Mary Chadwick entered the house. Rainy had been tempted to join her when the social worker asked her to foster Mikie, at least temporarily.

The needs of the other four already kept her hopping, but how could she refuse? The little boy broke her heart with his quivering lips and proud, stubborn chin. No matter how crowded her house or how busy her schedule, Mikie needed someone to care. Caring for needy children was what God had called her to do.

She took Mikie into the boys' bedroom for introductions, making sure Will and Josh helped him feel welcome. Both boys went immediately to the closet for the air mattress and began to set up an area of the room for the newcomer. They'd been through this drill before.

The telephone rang. She grabbed it on the second ring. "Hello."

"Rainy? Guy Bartlett. How are you and the Brady Bunch?"

She twined the cord around her finger. "Wild and crazy as always. How are you?" And why are you calling?

The thought was short-circuited by Guy's next words. "Look, I was thinking. We had a good time that day after church. I was wondering if you might like to do it again? Just me and you without the kids."

Oh dear. Maybe he did want to be more than friends. A dozen thoughts filtered through her head. He was a good Christian active in her church. He liked kids. There was no real reason for her not to go out with him, and yet, she didn't want to. How did she say no without hurting a nice man?

"Um, things are hectic right now, Guy. I'll have to say no."

A short paused ensued. "Another time then? Maybe next week?"

His obvious disappointment made her feel horrid, so she said, "Let's talk about it later, okay?"

She needed some time to figure a way to let him down easy.

Another pause and then, "Sure. See you at church?"

Rainy forced a smile into her voice. "Absolutely."

She'd no more than replaced the receiver when the phone rang again. Hoping it wasn't Guy with an alternative suggestion, she answered cautiously. "Hello."

"Hey, Slick," a dark, smooth baritone intoned. "My brownies are all gone."

At Nate's voice, Rainy couldn't ignore the leap of pleasure shooting through her veins. Funny how Nate had that effect and Guy didn't. "Are you a little piggie like my boys?"

"Oink, oink."

While she laughed and talked, Rainy absently used her sock-covered foot to dust the telephone table. Dust had a way of sneaking up on her. "Thanks for calling. I needed a laugh."

"Bad day?"

"Not bad as much as hectic." She told him about the social worker, Katie's persistent screams and the new boy. "To top it all off, we had a visit from our favorite police officer. Seems Katie's screams, even with the social worker on the premises, receive a lot of attention."

"Your neighbor again? What did you do to the woman, anyway?"

Carrying the cordless with her, Rainy checked to be sure Mikie was settling in. Will, bless him, solemnly rearranged a dresser drawer for the boy's meager belongings while Joshua plied Mikie with a handheld video game.

"Mrs. Underkircher is raising her only grandson alone and tends to spoil him a bit too much. He earned a low grade on his report card because he hadn't turned in a single assignment for over a month, even though I'd telephoned the home several times to discuss the problem. The low grade kept him off the honor roll. Which kept his name out of the local paper. Which caused him to be teased by another student."

"Woman, you should have your teaching license revoked."

Seeing that the children were okay, Rainy wandered into her bedroom for a few minutes of privacy and flopped onto a stack of seldom-used reading pillows. After teaching all day, attending a parent-teacher conference for Joshua and taking Katie to counseling, she was fried. Add the events of the last two hours and she was lucky to be breathing.

"Kathy Underkircher would agree."

"I was kidding."

Rainy stared at a cobweb above her bed. The fluffy little balls of dust were startling in the sunlight. Maybe she should shut the blinds. Instead, she looked around the room for something that would reach the ceiling, settling on a yardstick she used to measure the kids.

"I know you were joking. Unfortunately, Mrs. Underkircher isn't." She cradled the phone between her shoulder and chin and took a swing at the cobweb. "Somehow her vendetta turned personal. She claims I think too highly of myself, like I'm a saint or something because I take in foster kids."

"You are."

"Oh yes, Saint Rainy. This from the man who saw me totally freaked out over a flooded washing machine. And who has no idea that I'm trying to rid my ceiling of a giant cobweb at this very moment."

Crouching, she jumped and took another swing. "Missed again."

Nate's warm chuckle lifted her spirits. In fact, just hearing from him today after yesterday's impromptu, uninvited puppet show, thrilled her. Despite his occasional moodiness, she liked Nate Del Rio. She couldn't quite put her finger on the problem. He seemed to like the children, but he also seemed uptight with them at times.

She jumped again.

"Got it!" she shouted and then cringed. "Oops, sorry about the eardrum."

"No problem. I have another one."

Rainy giggled and fell back onto the fluffy lavender comforter. Right then and there she made a decision.

Nate probably hadn't been around kids much. That was why he didn't quite know how to react to them. That's why he was edgy at times and worried too much.

He just needed more exposure.

Nate didn't know for certain who started the phone calls, but he thought he might have been the guilty party. At the time, he must have been delirious on her double-dose brownies. That's the only excuse he could come up with for doing such a dumb thing. He thumped his head on the palomino's saddle, then mounted up. Somehow talking to Rainy on a daily basis had become a habit. One he looked forward to with growing enthusiasm.

Then yesterday morning he'd found himself standing on her front porch in the bright spring sunshine, red toolbox in hand as he dismantled her raucous-rock-band doorbell. Red tulips merrily mocked him from either side of the porch. Inside the house someone was playing a video game with sound effects. Next thing he knew, he was surrounded by kids jabbering away about school projects.

He'd been ambushed.

Now here they were again.

Holding the horse's reins at waist level with one hand, he leaned down to open the gate. Leather groaned and shifted as he rose in the stirrups, waiting for five more horses to plod past and out into open pasture on their first official trail ride.

With Nate riding alongside, Pop—with Katie stuck to his back like Velcro—led the single file parade. Rainy brought up the rear with Emma. The boys, including a newcomer named Mikie, rode in between.

Sweat broke out on Nate's neck. Pop and Rainy had talked him into this ride yesterday when she and the kids had driven out with a chocolate pie as thanks for fixing the doorbell. The pie was awesome, but he hadn't slept three hours last night thinking about all the things that could go wrong today.

They followed a well-trodden path made by the cows in numerous trips between the barn and the pond and beyond. Yo-Yo trotted alongside, his eyes bright and happy, his red tongue quivering in and out of his mouth.

Nate kept his attention roving from horse to horse and all around in search of hazards. As such, he caught the three boys watching him intently. With amused pride, Nate realized they were imitating him, each one sitting tall, reins in one hand, trying to perfect the cowboy posture. The difference was in relaxation. While Nate rode with one hand resting against his thigh, each boy gripped the saddle horn with a ferocity born of inexperience. As a result, they bounced like stiff little bobbleheads.

"Loosen the reins a little, like this," he said to Will, the closest to him.

Will nodded, serious as a heart attack, and adjusted his grip.

"This is supposed to be fun." A bug buzzed past his face. Nate swatted the air, coming up empty. "Relax and enjoy yourself."

"I am."

Yeah, right, Nate thought. Sweat beaded on Will's upper lip. The boy wrinkled his nose in an effort to adjust his sliding glasses and shot concerned looks toward his brother and sister. The kid didn't know how to relax. He always expected the worst.

Just like you.

The thought came out of nowhere and Nate shook it off. He didn't need his overactive sense of responsibility to horn in today.

He guided the group around the pond, where they spotted a pair of soft-eyed deer and a half dozen flapping, quacking ducks. The kids were excited to silence, a minor miracle to Nate's thinking.

He turned in the saddle. Rainy watched, too, both the animals and the children, with a gentle expression. She looked at him and mouthed, "Thank you."

Nate touched the brim of his hat, buoyed by that simple acknowledgment.

Maybe this wasn't so bad after all.

They rode farther into the pasture, over a ridge and into a shadowy line of woods along the creek. Nate wanted Rainy to see the area, certain she would appreciate its springtime beauty.

Dogwoods bloomed white and popcorn-like next to maroon redbud trees. Along the squishy, leaf-strewn riding path, bluebirds flashed in and out of blossoming limbs and sang in preparation for nesting. Tiny white and purple flowers jutted from the dark, damp earth. The smell was heady—green and moist and clean with nature's rebirth, yet ripe with the natural order of decay.

This was why he lived in the country and ranched. Days outdoors filled his spirit and soothed his troubles. He felt closer to God here than any other place on earth.

He glanced toward Rainy, wondering if she saw and felt what he did. Riding in and out of the leaf-dappled sunshine, her clear, pretty face was partly in shadow. She looked right and left, up and down, observing, listening to nature's wonder. When she took a deep breath and sighed, he had his answer. The notion that she, too, saw what he did filled a hollow longing beneath his ribcage. He didn't know why, couldn't begin to explain, but he relaxed in the saddle, content.

A low bawling sound broke the contemplative mood. Nate reined in the palomino. The horse tilted his head, listening, too. Yo-Yo paused in the trail, ears pricked up. The sound came again, high and plaintive, the cry of a calf. In two beats, the black and white cow dog hunkered low to the ground and, with a rustle of leaves, disappeared into the underbrush to fulfill his inborn job of protecting livestock.

"Better check that out, son," Pop said, riding up beside him. "Want me to go on ahead with our guests?"

They'd had their share of calves caught in barbed-wire fences, stuck in mud holes, or simply separated from mama. With coyotes always on the lookout for the young or weak, Nate took no chances with his registered stock.

By now, the other horses gathered around him.

"What is it, Nate?" Rainy asked. She looked like a rhinestone cowgirl in her fancy boots, jeans and a pink glittery vest. He'd plopped one of his hats on her head to make her laugh, and she'd amused—and pleased—him by wearing it.

"Probably a lost calf. Ride in easy so we don't spook him." He spoke as much to the children as to her. They all nodded their understanding.

"We gots to find her, Nate," Emma said, her blue eyes huge in her sun-kissed face. "Babies shouldn't never be without mamas. They get sad and cry."

The parallel between her situation and that of the calf was not lost on Nate. A lump formed in his throat. With a click of his tongue, he tapped Moccasin's flanks and rode on ahead.

By now, Yo-Yo had discovered the calf's whereabouts and yipped his find. Nate followed the sounds, his heart dropping to discover a mother and a newborn calf lying on the ground, the cow far too still.

Motioning to Rainy to wait with the children, he and Pop dismounted and approached the animals.

"Calf's brand new. Still wet."

"Mama's not looking so good."

Grimly, Nate flipped over her ear tag, discovering, as he feared, that she was one of his inseminated cows. The cow made no attempt to rise or protect her calf, both the norm, and he knew she wouldn't make it. Disappointment was a bitter taste in his mouth. He wasn't in this business to lose cows—especially now, when every penny counted.

The rustle and squeak of horses and leather brought his head up. His company dismounted, solemn and staring, to form a circle of mourning around the dying cow and her shivering black calf.

"Can we help?" Rainy asked softly.

He started to refuse and to send her and the children back to the house, but one look around the quiet circle changed his mind. "Why don't you fan out and gather dry leaves and grass for this little guy?"

As if the kids instinctively understood the need for stillness, they crept away, their colorful cowboy boots barely making a rustle on the soft grass.

By the time they returned, hands filled, the mother cow had heaved her last breath and Pop had headed back to the barn for the Mule. Nate felt as if someone had stepped on his chest. A registered Angus cow was worth a great deal of money. All he could do now was hope to save the calf.

The children gathered around him, uncertain. Their eyes gleamed with sadness and the need to do something helpful.

Swallowing his own dismay, Nate motioned to them. "Come on. Baby here is waiting. Keep your voices down and be as calm as you can."

"What are we going to do?" Rainy asked, holding out her clump of dried grass. "Feed this to him?"

"City slicker," he said with a tiny smile, glad for the bit of humor. "He's too young to eat grass. We dry him. Warm him up, stimulate his circulation." He motioned toward the oldest boy. "Will, you and Emma bring yours and rub this side. We'll take turns."

Amazingly, the children did exactly as they were told with a minimum of noise and commotion. After a bit of rubbing, the wobbly calf struggled to stand, a good sign. Nate caught him around the chest and head, holding him still while the others rubbed the black fur to a dull softness.

"Can we name him?" Joshua asked. "He's a nice cow."

"He's not a cow," Nate corrected. "He's a bull, a boy."

"Oh." Joshua patted the calf's neck. "He's a nice bull. Can we name him?"

Nate made a habit of never naming livestock, other than for registration purposes. Sentimentality had no place in the cattle business. "Cattle usually get numbers, not names."

"Oh." Joshua's lips turned down. His small, dirty hand swiped uselessly at the bits of hay and grass clinging to his zippered fleece jacket.

Nate shifted on his boots, his glance moving from the small worried faces to Rainy and back to the hapless calf. The kids had gathered around the newborn, fingers trailing over him, reluctant to release their collective support. Dried but still trembling, the orphaned animal rolled big, brown eyes, and Nate was done in.

"Considering this little fella's been through a rough time, I guess you could name him if you wanted to."

Five heads snapped upward. "We can?"

Rainy's smile was warm and alive with approval. "Nate, that's so nice."

If she kept looking at him that way, her eyes all soft and glowy, he'd let the kids name every cow on the place.

"Will he get a new mama?" Emma asked, worry raising crinkles beneath her blond bangs.

Rainy placed a hand on the child's head, her smile fading to bittersweet. In one of their lengthy phone calls, she'd told him of Emma's fixation on mothers. She'd also told him of her hope to adopt the siblings and Katie, although all four were legal risk adoptions. Frankly, he thought Rainy was nuts for putting herself in a position to get her heart broken.

"Pop and I will have to be his mama."

This brought a round of giggles and snickers.

To cheer them, Nate turned an index finger toward himself in mock insult. "What? I don't look like a mama to you?"

While the other children laughed, Joshua rushed in to reassure. "Maybe not a mama, but you'd make a real good daddy."

Nate mentally flinched. Poor Joshua had no idea how wrong he was. Nate had been a dad all his life and he was lousy at it. Just last night, he'd been on the telephone for an hour trying to bail Blake out of another scrape. No matter how hard he tried, his siblings couldn't seem to get their lives together.

He was glad Rainy and her kids didn't know what a failure he was.

The calf bawled again and Pop rode up on the Mule, cutting off any need to respond. Thankful for the interruption, Nate loaded the now-squirming calf onto the vehicle for conveyance back to the barn.

Rainy touched his arm. "I have an idea."

He turned, dusting his hands down the sides of his jeans. "Trying to scare me?"

He wasn't joking.

Rainy bumped him with her side. "Don't say that. Hear me out. Will and Joshua joined the 4-H program at school. They've been trying to decide on a project for the fair next fall. Why not let them take care of the calf as their project? They could help you and, in the process, learn about ranching and animal care."

Nate could think of a thousand reasons why he shouldn't agree. Over the roar of the departing Mule, he started with one. "The calf has to be cared for every day. Fed at least twice a day."

"If you and Pop could handle the morning feeding, the boys could ride the bus to the ranch each day after school. I'd be happy to pick them up later." She hooked an elbow around the neck of each boy and pulled them close. "Being responsible for an animal is an excellent way to build self-esteem and integrity and all kinds of good qualities. An animal project would really be a good thing for them to do."

She looked so full of hope and good intentions. When Will and Joshua added their enthusiastic promises to be the best calf mamas ever, Nate felt his resistance slipping away. He knew he'd be sorry. He knew it was a bad idea. But, with a pull of dread in his gut, he gave in.

Ambushed again.

Chapter Seven

Rainy sat on an upturned bucket inside a barn stall watching Joshua and Will groom and feed the growing calf. All in all, Rainy thought the project was one of her best ideas yet.

Dubbed BlackJack because of his smooth black coat, the calf had grown from a spindly-legged orphan into a sturdy, friendly youngster in six weeks' time.

Joshua and Will had made up in enthusiasm what they lacked in knowledge, listening well when Nate or Pop taught them something new about livestock. Will, who had never enjoyed reading, had begun checking out library books on the topic and scoured the Internet for ways to turn BlackJack into a prize show calf.

Things were going well, indeed.

As part of their project, the boys were required to keep a daily record book, complete with photos. Every day after tending BlackJack, Will and Joshua took turns meticulously logging information. Everything from the amount and type of milk replacer to how much the calf weighed went into the book.

Today, Rainy had brought her camera for some photo updates. As she raised the digital, an overeager BlackJack butted hard at his bottle and sent Joshua onto his backside.

Foamy milk suds encircled the calf's mouth like shaving cream as he nudged at his human mama to get up and feed him some more. Rainy snapped a photo.

The cute shot got even better when Will flopped onto the hay-strewn floor, laughing.

"Mad calf, mad calf," he managed between bursts of laughter. "He's foaming at the mouth."

Rainy had few photos of Will in such a joyful moment so she snapped away, thrilled to see him behave like a normal, fun-loving fifth-grader. This project was good for him in more ways than she had ever imagined. During her months of caring for Will, he had not begun to relax until these weeks with BlackJack.

Outside in the corrals, Nate and Pop were "working cows," whatever that meant. A handful of high school boys from the agriculture program had been hired to assist. If the shouts and moos and thumps of bovine bodies in the metal chutes were any indication, the critters weren't too happy about being "worked."

Curious, she took a couple more shots of the boys with BlackJack and then left them to their job, going to the barn door. Directly across from where she stood, a cowboy herded an animal into a narrow passage. Then three other workers converged on the bawling creature with syringes, ear tags and tubes of medication. Dust and dirt swirled around the noisy activity.

Yo-Yo, the happy collie, snaked around the legs of calves, adding a nip here and there to make a rowdy one behave or move him forward in the chutes.

Camera dangling from her arm, Rainy raised a hand to shade her eyes, spotting Nate in the midst of the commotion. Broad-shouldered and handsome in a gray shirt, he shoved a final calf into the head gate. The trap door clanged into place. He made a notation on a clipboard.

Rainy stood still, enjoying the view.

The evening trip to Crossroads Ranch had become her favorite part of the day. And Nate Del Rio was the reason.

Funny that she found him, a country boy, so fascinating. But Nate was more than a ruggedly handsome face. Smart and responsible, funny and kind, Nate's heart was as soft as a warm marshmallow. He just didn't want anyone to know it.

He'd admitted how much he enjoyed volunteering for the Handyman Ministry, but he was a pushover with the kids, too. He'd also formed a habit of checking the oil in her car every week even though she could do the task herself. When she'd tried to compliment him for the kindness, he'd made some joking comment about women mechanics.

She raised her digital and snapped.

He looked up, lifted his hat in greeting.

Rainy's heart fluttered crazily. She waved, and Nate said something to Pop, who nodded. Then Nate leaped over the steel corral and headed her way, shedding a pair of leather gloves in transit. Yo-Yo spotted his master's departure and slithered beneath an iron gate to follow.

Okay, so she liked Nate. A lot. The more time she spent with him, the more she liked him. They were friends, but she wouldn't mind if they were more. Sometimes she thought he felt the same. At other times, she wasn't so sure. But something was going on between them.

The kids thought Nate was the coolest dude on the planet.

Maybe Rainy thought so, too.

Maybe there was hope for an old maid schoolteacher with four foster kids. They'd never exactly discussed Nate's stand on the subject of foster care and adoption, but he must be agreeable. He was letting the boys foster BlackJack. That had to count for something.

While her thoughts tumbled around, Nate sauntered

toward her in the sunshine, his dusty boots striding in that easy cowboy manner that had her wondering why she'd never noticed cowboys before Nate. Her mouth titled upward. She was noticing now.

"Hey, Slick, what's up?" he asked. He rubbed a bandana over his sweaty face, stuck the red cloth in his back pocket and grinned. His killer dimples made an appearance, setting off the laugh lines around his eyes.

"Same old same old, Cowboy," she answered.

Their nicknames for one another had stuck, and Rainy had to admit she liked hers. She even liked being teased for some of the silly questions she asked about cows and horses and ranching.

She snapped another photo, earning a mock scowl. He reached out and slid the camera from her wrist. "My turn."

Rainy protested, ducking to one side when he raised the digital. "No way."

He laughed and snapped. "Smile pretty or suffer the consequences."

She made a face. He snapped again. This time she burst out laughing. He snapped that, too.

"I want a copy of every one of them."

"No way."

"You're repeating yourself." He took her hand and slid the camera strap onto her wrist. His fingers were calloused and rough against her tender skin, but his touch was light and easy. A zing of energy flooded her. Being in Nate's company had that effect.

They stood in the entry to the barn for several long seconds, saying nothing, grinning at each other. Nate leaned a shoulder against one of the doorposts.

Rainy took the other doorpost, bending a knee to prop her foot against the barn. From this spot, she could hear the boys and enjoy the sunshine with Nate.

"Riding the Mule yesterday was fun," she said.

A red wasp buzzed close. Using his hat, he slapped the insect to the ground, then smashed it with his boot toe. "We'll have to do it again sometime."

"I'd like that."

He'd taken turns giving rides to all of them, but hers had been the longest. She'd loved every minute of sitting next to Nate while they rumbled across the green grass. With four children around, time alone was not to be taken lightly.

"I got some news today." He replaced the Stetson, adjusting the brim low over his eyes.

"Good news?" she asked, not sure what this had to do with riding the ATV.

"I think so." He hitched his chin toward a fence line in the distance. "That land over there where we rode the Mule."

"Your leased property?" With a quiet intensity she hadn't completely understood, he'd detailed the eight hundred acres as they drove by ponds and a creek, stands of timber and loading chutes. His black Angus cattle roamed fat and content in the long, open areas of lush, green Bermuda grass.

"Right now I'm only leasing half. The lease runs out at the end of this year, but I have an option to buy the entire acreage. This morning I talked to the owner."

"He's ready to sell?"

Nate nodded. "He moved to South Dakota several years ago, so I've been expecting this. But Pierson was clear about one thing. He needs the money to invest in his business. So if I don't buy the property, he'll sell to someone else. He already has other offers."

She could see the prospect worried him. "Are you going to buy it, then?"

"I want to. I've wanted to for a long time. Buy the land. Add another hundred head of cattle." His face shone with quiet excitement. Rainy saw past the casual words to the dream inside. "I'm starting to believe I can make it happen."

"Sounds like a huge investment."

He nodded. "I knew sooner or later Pierson would sell, so I've been saving the down payment for a while. In the ranching business, a man either has to go big or keep grubbing with the small stuff. I want Crossroads Ranch to become the premiere organic beef ranch in this part of the state."

"Organic? That's awesome, Nate." Pushing off the door, she dropped her foot to the hard-packed earth. "I can see it now. Restaurants advertising organic steaks and burgers from Crossroads Ranch. Healthy and delicious."

Pleased amusement played around his lips. He joined her in the center of the entry and tugged her hair. "Thanks for the vote of confidence, Slick. I hope you're right."

Rainy hoped she was right, too. To her way of thinking, an honest Christian guy like Nate was good for the business world.

"I'd better check on the boys. They should be finished by now." They started walking that direction, taking their time, lazily enjoying one another's company.

"They're turning into good little ranch hands," Nate said, and there was pride and affection in his admission. "I can leave them alone with BlackJack now, knowing they can handle him."

They'd come a long way, indeed. "Think they'll win a prize at the fair?"

"Too early to tell. BlackJack's still a baby, but he's from good stock."

"Will the fact that he's bottle raised hurt him?"

"Some calves don't fare as well, but as I said, Will and Josh are trying to compensate. BlackJack should do fine."

"You've taught them a lot."

"Will comes in every day with some new idea he's read somewhere. If I'm not careful, he'll run me out of business one of these days." The quick flash of dimples showed he was teasing.

"You wouldn't believe his aversion to books before Black-Jack. Before coming into the social system, he didn't attend school regularly, so reading is hard for him. He also didn't see any value in reading until now."

"You're good for them. They're thriving."

Happiness spread through Rainy like a smile on the inside. Nate had the uncanny ability to say the right things.

"I hope the courts agree."

"Are you worried about that? About them being taken away?"

She shrugged one shoulder, tilting her head. "I try not to."

"But you do."

"Yes, I do. I know I shouldn't. God has a plan for their lives. I don't want my wants to ever get in the way, but I've bonded with all four of these kids. Losing them would hurt."

"Would you ever give it up?" he asked, pausing just inside the shaded building. "Doing foster care, I mean."

There was something intense in the way he asked, some unspoken meaning that gave Rainy pause, made her wonder. She couldn't quite figure out what he meant.

She turned around then, looking back out at the pasture where calves kicked and bucked, in a hurry to rejoin their waiting mothers. Sometimes she wondered if her foster children felt that pull toward their birth mothers. Surely they did. They must. But they loved her, too. She was the person who'd provided the stable, loving, Christian home none of them had ever had before.

"Fostering is hard sometimes," she said, turning back to face him. "Dealing with the uncertainty, the heartaches. But I can't imagine a life without children."

A nameless emotion shifted over Nate's face. He glanced away, swallowed.

"That's what I thought," he said softly, as if to himself.

Rainy studied the side of his face, the strong jaw, the dimple creases she liked so much. For some strange reason, she felt as if he'd given her a test...and she'd failed.

Without another word, Nate headed deeper into the barn. Following behind, Rainy kicked a loose dirt clod at him. "Hey, Cowboy, did I do something?"

Nate looked over his shoulder. "Nah. Not you. Me. Come on. Time for the boys to muck out the stall. You gotta get a picture of that."

Though Rainy couldn't shake the feeling that she'd done something wrong, she let the subject drop. Side by side, she and Nate leaned their arms atop the stall's half door and peered at the scene inside. His elbow bumped hers. She tried to ignore the touch, concentrating instead on Will and Joshua.

The scent of fresh straw, bedding material for the calf, filled her nostrils. The little calf followed the boys around, nudging at them with friendly affection. Occasionally, Joshua or Will stopped working long enough to scratch BlackJack behind the ears. Yo-Yo belly crawled toward Josh, nudging with his black nose.

Nate tilted his head toward hers. "Where are blondie and the screamer today?"

Mikie had long since been returned to his mother and Rainy prayed every night that she'd embrace this second chance, stay away from her abusive boyfriend and make a good home for Mikie.

"Birthday party. A little girl from church." She checked her watch. "Don't let me forget to leave by six-thirty. The party is over at seven."

Pop appeared in the alleyway between the stalls and outside, his round, weathered face shaded by the broad-brimmed Stetson.

"We got company." He jerked a thumb toward the house. "Other than Rainy, I mean. She's homefolks now."

Rainy straightened, thanking him for the kind sentiment with a smile.

"Who is it?" Nate pushed away from the stall, dusting his hands down his jeans as he went to join his grandfather. Rainy followed the pair back out into the sunlight.

"Don't recognize the truck," Pop said. "But the driver looks like Janine."

Janine? Rainy frowned. Who was that?

She started to ask but noticed the tight line of Nate's mouth and changed her mind. Maybe later. A lot later.

A battered gray pickup truck came to a dust-stirring halt in the driveway beside the house. A young woman with a baby in her arms stepped out and came toward them. Richly tanned, with long, dark, curly hair and an ultra-slim figure beneath a black and white polka-dot sundress, the newcomer looked pretty enough to turn heads.

Rainy glanced at Nate to see if his was one of them.

It wasn't. Still bristling like a threatened cat, he made an unhappy sound in the back of his throat.

"Excuse me," he said tersely, his eyes locked on the woman and baby. "I'll be back."

He strode off to meet the newcomer.

Rainy knew she was nosy to listen in, but she couldn't seem to help herself. After Nate's odd reaction to the woman's arrival, she was curious. Maybe a little jealous, too. Nate had never mentioned any old girlfriends.

Nate's palomino edged a nose over the wire fence and whickered. Rainy sauntered close to stroke his velvety muzzle, an excuse, she admitted, to stay within hearing distance without appearing too obvious.

Voices from the driveway carried on the breeze. The woman's rose, strident and insisting. "I need the money, Nate."

Nate removed his hat and tapped it against his thigh. The baby, a girl, reached toward him. He jiggled her tiny hand with his free one. The baby's toothless smile rewarded him, but Nate turned a concerned gaze on the woman.

By now, Will and Joshua had finished their chores and came to stand beside her at the fence. Feeling a little foolish, she was glad for their company.

"Who is that lady, Miss Rainy?"

"I don't know, Will." Not that Nate's company was any of her business, but she shamelessly tried to hear the conversation. Nate looked so troubled.

Unwanted thoughts raced through her head. Her heart sank. Who *was* this demanding woman with the adorable baby?

To her embarrassment, Pop must have noticed her curiosity. He joined her at the fence.

"That's Janine," he said without preamble. "Nate's sister. Wonder what she wants?"

With relief, Rainy now saw the family likeness. No wonder Janine was darkly pretty. "She's lovely. Is that her baby?"

"Yep. Little Bailey. Cute as a new kitten. Come on. I'll introduce you."

"Nate doesn't look like he wants company."

"Ah, he's all right. Come on. We might keep him out of trouble."

Shoving her fingertips into her back pockets, Rainy fell into step beside the rancher. "Keep him out of trouble? How?"

"I guess he hasn't told you much about his family."

"Just that his parents are dead and he has a brother and a sister. I can tell he worries about them a lot."

Pop snorted. "Too much, if you ask me, which you didn't, but I'm telling you anyway. He has some fool notion that he's the only one who can take care of them. Janine and Blake know how he feels and take advantage." He took a hitch at his jeans and sniffed. "Don't tell him I said that. He's touchy about it. Janine's a good girl, sweet as pie, but spoiled rotten and doesn't have a lick of common sense. Nate lets her get to him."

Rainy wasn't surprised. Nate was a born softy. "He cares about her."

"It's a whole lot more than caring. That's the bad thing about the whole mess." As they drew closer to Nate and Janine, Pop lifted a hand. "Quiet now. Don't want him knowing I said anything."

Rainy wondered about Pop's curious observation but she was so relieved that Janine was a sibling instead of a girl-friend that she didn't dwell on Pop's meaning.

Their boots crunched on the loose gravel. Nate must have heard because he turned, one hand on his hip, a scowl on his brow.

Pop made the introductions. "Let's all go inside and have a good visit," he said. "Janine and Rainy can get acquainted."

Nate's scowl deepened.

Janine shook her head. Loose, pretty curls danced around her shoulders. "Next time, Pop. Today I have to run. Nate and I have a little business to take care of first. You all go on inside without us."

Rainy recognized a brush-off when she saw one, but Pop said, "Nah, that's okay. We'll wait."

Nate narrowed a look at his grandfather. "Pop."

"Okay, okay." Pop kissed the babbling baby on the forehead and hugged Janine. "Talk to you later. Me and these cowpokes are hankering for a long, tall glass of sody water anyways. Isn't that right, boys?"

Oblivious to the undercurrent between adults, Will and Joshua grinned.

Rainy started to follow the boys inside, but Nate's voice turned her around. "Rainy."

He never called her that. "Yes?"

"You're not leaving yet, are you?"

She glanced at her watch. "Soon."

The baby in Janine's arms patted Nate's shoulder. He took her into his arms. At the sight of Nate holding a small baby, a funny feeling settled beneath Rainy's ribs.

"I rented a movie," he said, heedless of the baby tugging at his ear. "Thought you might like it."

She smiled. "Oh yeah? What's the movie?"

"A surprise. Come tomorrow prepared to stay. I'll even feed you."

"Feed me? As in pizza delivery, or home cooking?"

"Come and find out. You might be surprised."

Her smile widened. "I'll be here."

The next afternoon Nate hit the shower earlier than usual, and then dressed in clean jeans and shirt. Later, he'd whip up a Tex-Mex casserole to pop in the oven before Rainy and the children arrived. He couldn't wait to see her expression when she discovered he was a pretty fair cook. No pizza delivery for him.

"What are you getting all spiffed up for?" Pop limped in through the back door and tossed his hat on the couch.

"No use smelling like a cow lot just because I'm in the ranching business." He reached for Pop's white Stetson and hung the battered straw on a hook by the back door. "Why are you limping?"

"Cow stepped on my foot." Pop pulled two kitchen chairs face to face, collapsed in one with a gusty sigh and propped his boot on the other. "And don't change the subject. You never fancy up in mid afternoon."

"Nosy old man."

"I'd thump your head for disrespect if I didn't know you was joking." Pop eased his boot off, letting it fall to the floor with a thud. Dirt spattered the floor in a starburst. His big toe poked through a hole in a white tube sock. "You are joking, ain't you?"

"Sorry, Pop. You know I am."

"Good. Now tell me what's going on. Going somewhere?"

"Rainy's coming over."

"Comes over every day." Pop peeled the sock away with a grimace. The top of his foot was blue and puffy. With a knowing expression, he squinted toward Nate. "You like her, don't you?"

"We're friends. What's not to like?" Nate shrugged, turning his attention to Pop's injured foot. "That looks bad. Want me to run you in to the doctor's office?"

"Nah. Just a bruise. Hazard of the business." He motioned toward the sink. "Get me a bucket of hot water. A good soaking will fix me right up."

"Uh, Pop. Do you mind soaking somewhere else?" Nate rubbed the back of his neck, thinking of the dirt from Pop's boots. Now he'd have to clean the floor again. "Rainy's staying for dinner. And a movie. I'm cooking in here."

His grandfather leaned back in his chair and grinned what could only be termed a "possum-eatin'" grin.

"As in a date?"

Nate shrugged.

"Well now, if that isn't an answer to prayer, I don't know what is."

Nate narrowed his eyes in what he hoped was a warning look. "Meaning?"

Pop chuckled. "Sounds like more than friends to me. And I'm mighty glad to hear it. The Word says a man ought not to be alone. Needs a helpmate."

"You're alone."

"But I had your granny for a lot of good years. You keep floundering around, you'll miss out on all the good ones. I can tell you, Nate boy, Miss Rainy's a good one."

Nate couldn't argue that, but they did have one major problem. And he saw no way around it. "She wants to adopt kids."

"Nothing wrong with wanting young ones. That's one of the things that makes her special, shows what a fine woman she is."

"I wouldn't mind finding a wife, but I've had kids all my life. I'm done with that."

"You've had a set of pain-in-the-neck, overindulged siblings."

"Same thing."

"They're adults now, son. The sooner you let them grow up, the sooner you can think of yourself instead of taking care of them."

"I can't just turn them out like yearling calves. Not when they need my help."

"What do you need, Nate boy? You're not getting any younger or better looking. You got needs, too. Get to thinking on that for a change."

Pop's attempt at humor sailed right past him.

"What I need doesn't matter, Pop. You know what happened the one time I turned my back." His stomach started to churn in that old familiar way. "You *know* why I can't ever refuse them."

Pop studied him with a compassion Nate resented. He didn't deserve anyone feeling sorry for him. What happened had been his fault.

Pop laid his dirty sock across his knee and in a soft voice said, "Christine is gone, son. Martyring yourself won't bring her back."

The memory of his crucial decision, of his deepest, ugliest failure, jabbed into Nate like a hot knife. Pop knew better than to mention Christine. They never talked about her. Ever. Didn't he realize that Nate carried the guilt with him every moment of every day? Having her name shoved in his face, forced into conversation, was too much.

Swallowing back a groan of agony, he muttered, "I'll get that hot water."

He stalked to the sink and crouched to rattle around in the lower cabinet. The soft scuttle of chair and boot warned him of Pop's approach. The old man placed a hand on his shoulder.

"I didn't mean to upset you, Nate boy." He emitted a frustrated huff. "It's just...I want you to let go and be happy. That's all."

His shoulders were tight with tension, but Nate couldn't stay upset with his grandfather. For all his straight shooting, Pop cared deeply.

"Forget about it," he said, wishing he could. Wishing he could erase the wrong he'd done to his own sister. Wishing he could go back in time and change his response to that one phone call.

Digging an old blue dishpan from under the sink, he rose and stuck it beneath the faucet.

He couldn't change what he'd done to Christine. But he could take care of Janine and Blake. If that was his penance from God, he'd accept it. Even if it meant always being alone.

Chapter Eight

Rainy noticed a thin undercurrent of tension the moment she arrived at Crossroads Ranch. Nothing was said, and Pop was as jovial as always, but Nate seemed to have something on his mind. Rainy wondered if his mood had anything to do with Janine's visit the day before. She also wondered what Pop had meant when he'd said the siblings took advantage of Nate. Beneath all his cowboy macho, Nate had a soft heart, but she couldn't imagine anyone taking advantage of him without his permission.

"You two get the grub on the table," Pop said. "I'll go round up the boys." He pointed at Emma and Katie. "You cowgirls going with me?"

Emma batted long eyelashes. "Can we ride the four-wheeler?"

With a chuckle, Pop wagged his head. "Oh, I reckon so. Won't hurt nothing. As long as Katie here promises not to scream."

"She won't scream, will you, Katie?" Emma said, one small hand squeezing the other girl's upper arm.

Rust-colored freckles stood out against creamy, pale skin as Katie said, "Not if I can ride first."

Rainy's heart turned over every time she looked at her foster daughters. Emma was a sweetheart and, for all her difficulties, Kate was a precious little girl slowly learning to deal with life's frustrations with words instead of screams.

"Done!" Pop said with a chuckle and hustled the adorable pair out the back door.

Rainy went to the kitchen window and watched the trio cross the green grassy space between house and barn. She got more joy watching her little girls play than she had ever imagined possible. They were gifts from God, and she prayed they would be with her always.

"Is your granddad limping?"

Nate, busy assembling the ingredients for a green salad, glanced up. "Cow stepped on him."

"Ouch." Rainy turned away from the window to enjoy another sight—a cowboy in the kitchen. "What did the doctor say?"

"Pop hasn't been to a doctor in thirty years. He says bones heal whether a doctor says they're broken or not." With an affectionate twinkle in his eye, Nate stuck his chin out in a stubborn jut to imitate his grandfather. "God made 'em, He can fix 'em."

Rainy laughed and reached around him, snagging a piece of lettuce.

All day she'd looked forward to the evening with Nate. More than once, she'd had to remind herself that this was probably not a date, but nevertheless, she'd rushed home after school. Like a giddy teenager, she'd changed clothes three times before settling on a magenta pullover tucked into jeans with a wide, fancy belt. Because Nate teased her mercilessly about her girly footwear, she'd worn a pair of hot-pink heels just for fun.

"What smells so amazing?" she asked. A blend of tomato and spices had been driving her crazy since the moment she'd entered the warm, fragrant kitchen.

"That, Slick," Nate said, gesturing with a paring knife, "is the house specialty, beef enchilada casserole with sides of Spanish rice and refried beans."

"Who's the cook? Don Pueblos?"

One side of his mouth tipped up. He turned the point of the knife toward his chest. "Señor Del Rio. Me."

She backed against the kitchen counter, crossing her arms as she leveled him with a disbelieving stare. "No, seriously. You ordered out."

"Hey! I do not order out. A man who doesn't like frozen dinners or driving into town to eat learns to cook or starves. Starving is not cool. So I wanted to impress you with my culinary expertise."

"Color me impressed. I expected something much less domestic from a—" She stopped, grinning sheepishly at the sexist remark about to come out of her mouth.

Busy tossing the salad around with a fork and spoon, Nate paused mid-stir, clearly amused. "I know what you were thinking. A man, especially a rancher, shouldn't cook anything except barbeque on the grill."

"Or hot dogs over a campfire," Rainy joked as she pushed away from the cabinet and began to gather up loose bits of lettuce. "Sorry for the stereotype. I guess I'm an old-fashioned girl in a lot of ways. At my house, Mom always did the cooking and cleaning. Dad did the yard and took care of the car."

"And never the twain should meet?"

Lettuce scraps in hand, she glanced around for the trash can. Nate pointed toward the side of the refrigerator. Sometime since the day of the puppet show, he'd rearranged. Nate was, quite possibly, a neat freak about his house. Rainy wondered if he'd ever dusted furniture with his sock feet. Probably not.

"That's why I have to call the Handyman Ministry so often." Rainy stepped on the pedal and the silver trash can *thwanged* open. "Daddy wouldn't teach me anything he considered man's work. A boyfriend in college taught me to change the oil in my car, and Daddy got so mad. He said the boy was too lazy to do the job for me."

"Boyfriend, huh? You've never mentioned boyfriends before." He placed the glass salad bowl in the center of the table, the red and green vegetables creating a colorful contrast.

"You've never mentioned girlfriends before." Rainy dusted tiny bits of lettuce from her hands into the trash and then *thwanged* the lid shut again.

"Nope. I haven't." With that maddening answer, he motioned to an upper cabinet. "Mind setting the table?"

"Not at all." She touched a pull knob. "Plates in here?"

"Next one over."

She opened the door and counted down seven plain white plates rimmed in black. "Are my chocolate pecan bars going to fit into your fancy Tex-Mex menu? Or should I take them back home?"

He made a harrumphing noise. "Don't even think about it. You'll never escape this house with anything but an empty plate."

Rainy smiled on the inside. Nate had a way of making her feel good about her simple talents.

Astoundingly efficient in the kitchen, he slid bottled salad dressing and croutons onto the table with one hand while straightening chairs around the table with the other. Rainy could not imagine her father doing any of these things.

She wondered then about Nate's family. With his mother and father gone, did the others come here for holidays? Did Nate cook for them? And what *had* Pop meant when he'd said they took advantage?

To her way of thinking families were supposed to help each other. Even though her folks lived an hour away, she knew they were there if she needed them. Would Pop consider that taking advantage?

Nate's voice broke into her thoughts. "How can you bake sweets all the time and still look the way you do?"

"Is that a compliment?" she asked, preening a bit as she took plates to the table.

"Don't let it go to your head." When he opened the oven, a spicy, rich scent wafted forth. Rainy almost swooned.

"Too late. Already did. You paid me a compliment and here's one in return. You look nice, too. That emerald shirt turns your eyes green." Another reason to nearly swoon. Nate with green, green eyes above those dimples was breathtaking.

"Emerald?" He dipped his chin to his chest, pretending to stare at his shirt. "Is that what this is? I thought it was green."

"Ha. Very funny. Next you'll say my pullover is purple."

"It is."

"Magenta."

The oven door thudded shut. Nate moved closer, merriment in his expression, staring at her feet. "I suppose the shoes are magenta, too?"

"Nope," she said, enjoying the game. "Pink. Plain old pink."

With a grin and shrug, he said, "A man can't win."

"What fun would that be?"

They laughed into each other's eyes and the moment extended. Nate shifted slightly and Rainy had the lovely thought that he might kiss her. She'd thought it before, weeks ago, but the timing had been wrong. They hadn't really known each other then. Now she knew Nate as an honorable man who took relationships seriously. People mattered to him. Though he'd never said so, Rainy knew she mattered. The questions remained, how much and in what way?

She watched his eyes, mesmerized by the tenderness lurking in the green depths. Tenderness? For her?

A slight smile lingered on his lips, activating the dimples. He raised a hand, touched her cheek with the backs of his knuckles. Her heart fluttered, hopeful, expectant.

The oven timer *beep, beep, beeped.* They both jumped, and then laughed. With a wry expression, Nate turned away to answer the call.

A sliver of disappointment slid through Rainy.

She touched her fingertips to her cheek. Who would imagine a rough, tough cowboy could be so tender?

Just then, the back door banged open on its hinges. With an explosion of jovial noise, Pop and the four children clattered inside and the tender moment was lost forever as dinner was served.

But Rainy couldn't forget the caring look in Nate's eyes or the sudden burst of joy in her heart. When they bowed their heads to say grace, she struggled to keep her mind on the Lord and off the smooth rumble of Nate's baritone. A praying man was an enthralling attraction.

All through dinner she was acutely aware of him sitting across the table. Now and then, she'd look up from her plate to find him watching her, his expression interested and wondering. When he'd catch her staring—something she did far too often—he'd smile or wink and the expression disappeared.

After the meal and the dishes were cleared away, Rainy settled the children at the table to complete homework. As she did at home, she moved from chair to chair, helping each child. Will and Joshua, confirmed haters of homework, both grumbled and dawdled until Nate sat down between them.

"School's important, boys," he said quietly. "Don't give Rainy a hard time. She wants you to do well for *you,* not for her. She cares about your future. If you don't study hard and learn, life will be real tough when you grow up."

The two boys listened as if their lives depended on it. Then they bent their heads to the task and grumbled no more.

Gratitude filled Rainy. Will and Josh needed the counsel and example of a godly man. Rainy was more than glad that man was Nate Del Rio. Nate would make an awesome daddy.

There it was. A notion that had danced around the edges of Rainy's mind since that first day when Nate had rescued the children from the closet. Until this moment, she'd kept the thought hidden, forbidding it to bloom.

Even now, the revelation flustered her, made her all too aware of Nate's strong, masculine presence, of the dreams and longings she'd pushed aside, convinced they would never happen. She wanted to fall madly in love, not settle for anyone who would accept her and her kids. Her thoughts went to Guy Bartlett. After the last two turn-downs, he'd stopped calling, and she was relieved. Though she didn't begin to understand the reasons, she felt something with Nate that was missing with Guy and every other man. To escape her inner discomfort, Rainy leaned over Katie's shoulder and asked her to sound out the word *basket*.

Still, the idea wouldn't go away.

God must have a sense of humor, she thought, to let a city girl become enamored of a rancher, especially when that woman had given up on ever finding Mr. Right. She wasn't sure if Nate was the one, but the idea didn't scare her away.

Remembering his curious expression at dinner, she hoped the idea didn't scare *him* away, either.

When homework was nearly finished, Nate pushed back his chair and stood. "About ready for that movie I promised you?"

"I was starting to wonder if you'd made that up." She helped the smaller children stuff books and papers into their backpacks, then followed Nate into the living room.

"Check this out," he said, extending a DVD case. "Just for you."

"What is it?" She squinted toward the cover but couldn't make out the title. "A chick flick in my honor?"

He looked offended. "Not even close. I wouldn't be caught dead renting a chick flick."

Rainy laughed. "Oh, Cowboy, I'm going to make you eat those words. Give me that DVD."

She reached for it. Nate held the shiny plastic above his head, out of her reach. She jumped for it. He dipped to one side. Even in heels she didn't stand a chance against his superior height.

When he grinned like the ornery man he was, she slammed a fist onto her hipbone. "If you don't give me that right this minute, I'm going to do something terrible."

By now, Pop and the children had joined the fracas.

"Better give it to her, Nate," Will said. "She and Katie might start screaming."

"Me, too," said Emma, not to be left out.

As if terrified by the notion of three screaming females, Nate quickly deposited the DVD in Rainy's outstretched palm.

She looked down, read the title and started laughing. "*City Slickers?* Where in the world did you find this old movie?"

With a twitch of his eyebrows, Nate admitted, "I ordered it off the Internet. An edited version, especially for you."

Though secretly delighted to know Nate had been thinking about her enough to do such a cute thing, Rainy pretended insult. "You owe me, Cowboy."

"Ooh, I'm shaking." He extended both hands, giving an exaggerated tremble.

"Better be." She flexed a bicep, pointing at the pitiful bump. "Feel that muscle. Stainless steel."

Nate squeezed her upper arm, eyes widening in fun. "Dangerous. Mosquitoes beware."

With a head toss and a tiny sniff for good measure, Rainy settled onto the brown sofa next to Will while Nate set up the DVD player.

Will gave her a funny look, glancing from her to Nate. Then without a word, he moved to another chair. Nate, balanced on his toes in front of the TV, pivoted around, saw the only empty seat next to her and winked at Will. The boy grinned and hitched his chin toward Rainy in a not-so-subtle movement.

"What are you two up to?" she asked.

Nate scooted next to her on the sofa and pointed the remote toward the big screen. "No talking in the theater."

Will snickered.

"Good thing we're not in a theater." Rainy burrowed her shoulders deep into the couch cushions. The scent of Nate's clean cotton shirt followed her. "I love to talk."

"So I noticed."

"Hey!" She bopped him on the shoulder.

Nate captured her hand. Rainy stopped talking.

Why fight a good thing?

Though surrounded by kids, Nate was having a great time. He credited his good mood to Rainy, of course. Her reaction to the movie pleased him and he couldn't resist teasing her throughout.

The old comedy was about a group of city slicker friends who vacation on a working dude ranch and get into all sorts of funny situations. Some of the events paralleled a few of the blunders she and the children had made when first coming to Crossroads Ranch.

He thought her city girl mistakes were cute. Truth be told, he thought everything about Rainy was cute.

"Move over, Will. You're in my way." Emma shoved at her brother's shoulder.

Well, almost everything.

He liked the children. It wasn't that. Sometimes they hit him right in the heart. There lay his concern. He didn't need any more heart problems.

A scene played out across the television. A mama cow died birthing her calf. Katie sniffed. "Like BlackJack."

Rainy and Nate exchanged glances. They both knew Katie's response went far deeper than the orphaned calf.

A pinch of sadness dampened the laughter in Rainy's eyes. Nate stroked his thumb over the back of her hand, hoping to comfort her. He didn't know if it would, but Rainy's touch comforted him. The least he could do was return the favor.

Earlier in the kitchen, he'd thought about kissing her. Considering his ambivalent feelings toward her family, he shouldn't be thinking such a thing. But she made him smile and smelled so good, and her small, soft hand seemed tailor-made for him to hold.

Rainy was a strong, independent woman who didn't need anyone, but just the same, she made him feel necessary. Protective even. God-given male instinct, he supposed, but different from what he felt for Blake and Janine. He wasn't obligated to do things for Rainy; he wanted to do them.

She turned her attention back to the screen and giggled. The sound tickled Nate on the inside, like a bubble of happiness beneath his ribcage.

Miss Rainy was mighty distracting.

He should put an end to this budding infatuation before he fell in too deep. He should, but he didn't want to. Not yet, anyway.

The telephone jangled. Since Pop had disappeared into his bedroom to nurse the sore foot, Nate got up to answer, reluctantly loosing his hold on Rainy's hand.

As he reached for the wall phone, he glanced at the caller ID. Some of his pleasant mood leached away. Blake. His gut tightened.

"Is something wrong?" It was the first question he always asked. "Where are you? Are you all right?"

His grip tightening on the receiver, he turned his back and moved as far into the kitchen as possible. No use bothering Rainy with his problems. And his brother always seemed to have a problem.

"Sure, bro. Fine as frog hair. How are things at the ranch?"

Nate let out the breath he hadn't known he was holding. Maybe Blake's call wasn't another SOS. For all Nate's grousing, not every call was. Last week the two brothers had shared breakfast at the pancake house. Nate had paid, of course, but other than that, Blake had asked for nothing.

"Pop hurt his foot today, but he's tough." Nate recounted the situation, drawing a knowing laugh from Blake.

"I don't know how you put up with the old dude," his brother said. "Always preaching at you and waving the Bible under your nose."

Other than genetics, he and Blake had so little in common. "Don't start about Pop. If you'd listen to him, you'd be a lot better off."

In the adjoining living room, conversation began to flow again as the movie ended. He wanted to be in there with them, instead of standing here worrying about his adult brother.

When Rainy came into his life, she'd stirred up a lot of latent emotions. The jury was still out on whether that was a good thing or a bad one. Right now, he was enjoying his time with her more than anything he'd done in the last ten years. Maybe Pop was right. Maybe the time had come for him to focus on his own life for a change.

Shutting out the sound of Rainy's sweet laughter, he forced his attention to the call. If his brother wanted something, he wouldn't beat around the bush too long.

Sure enough, after about five minutes of useless chatter during which Nate's hopes rose, Blake got to the point. He wanted another loan. Nate closed his eyes in disappointment. His brother had a decent job. He should be doing well, but he lived far above his means and had a habit of buying into get-rich schemes that never panned out. From the occasional urgency of Blake's needs, Nate suspected he gambled, too, though Blake denied it, knowing his brother's aversion to the habit.

He hoped Blake stayed clear of illegal activities, but he couldn't be certain. That one worry was enough to wake Nate in the night and keep him handing over checks. Gambling debts of the wrong kind could get a man hurt.

A dozen times over, he'd tried to explain finance to his brother, but the advice only lasted until Blake's next payment was overdue. Sometimes Nate considered letting his brother lose his car or condo, but if he did, where would Blake go? How could he get to work? Blake had him by the conscience, and they both knew it.

Resentment bubbled up as hot as heartburn at the amount of money Blake requested this time. Nate would have to dip into his savings. Now, when he was so close to buying the Pierson land, the withdrawal would hurt.

He kept that information from his brother. Why bother? Blake cared nothing for this ranch.

Gritting his teeth, he agreed to meet Blake at the bank in the morning. He hung up the phone and leaned both hands on the kitchen counter to stare out into the darkness at the piece of property he wanted so badly. Would he always be saddled like a pack mule with his brother? Would Blake ever grow up?

Nate thought of a lesson in the Bible, though the story was foggy. Yet the words "my brother's keeper" rattled around in his head, weighing him down, obligating him.

"Is everything all right?" Rainy's voice came from behind him. He turned to find her standing close, her expression concerned.

"My brother," he said, rubbing both hands over his face

as if he could wipe away the constant strain of being the oldest.

"You say that as if there's something wrong." She took his hands in hers, and that simple act eased some of his tension. "Can I help?"

She helped simply by being here. But he said, "Blake needs to help himself."

"Your brother and sister depend on you a lot, don't they?"

He twitched a shoulder. "No big deal."

She didn't seem to buy his answer. "Was that why you were so tense when I first arrived this evening?"

So she'd noticed.

He wasn't about to open the Pandora's box containing his biggest mistake and watch Rainy's looks of admiration turn to disgust. Instead, he told her about Blake's inclination to overspend and to run to Nate for help.

The television rumbled in the background, but Rainy focused on him, saying nothing while he dumped his tale of woe on her slender shoulders.

When he finished, she only asked, "How old is Blake?"

The question took him aback. He blinked. "Twenty-nine, why?"

What did age have to do with anything?

Head bent, she studied their joined hands, as if searching for the right words. Nate gazed down at the crown of her head, admired the way her hair shone beneath the kitchen light. Everything about Rainy Jernagen shone, from the inside out.

He was aware of many things at that moment, as though his senses had heightened with Rainy in the room. The lingering scents of spicy Tex-Mex and soapy lemon dishwater. The taste of Rainy's chocolate bars on his tongue. The incredible softness of her skin against his. Even the quiet rhythm of her breathing.

After a long moment, she met his gaze and said, "Nate, *I'm* twenty-nine."

The flood of senses fled, replaced by bewilderment. Nate frowned. "I don't see your point."

Gently, carefully, she said, "Isn't Blake—and for that matter, Janine—old enough to handle his own finances without depending on you?"

Nate tugged his hands away, fisted them at his side, disappointed. He'd thought she would understand. "Our parents are dead. I'm the oldest."

Rainy's small, sad smile—a smile that never reached her eyes—confused him more. "You sound exactly like Will."

Was she judging him? Criticizing? He glanced over her shoulder to the living area, where Will and the other children watched TV. He didn't see the connection. She probably thought he came from a family of losers. Sometimes he thought the same thing, though she couldn't possibly comprehend what they'd all been through. What he had done to them.

"I'm all they have, Rainy."

"They have each other and Pop. Aren't they Christians?"

Her words were a gentle rebuke. At least, that's the way Nate perceived them. *He* had God to lean on. They didn't. He shoved a hand over his head, squeezed the back of his neck. On an exhale, he said, "Not yet. Pop and I are still praying."

She touched his shoulder in that soft way she had, gentle as a baby's, but her sweetness went all the way through him like a transfusion of honey. "I'll pray, too. I'll pray for you, as well, Nate. You're carrying a heavy load."

She had no idea. And Nate never intended for her to know the whole story. He liked her too much.

"You're carrying a pretty heavy load yourself." He looked toward the children sprawled around his living room. Next to the couch, Katie stood on her head while Emma steadied her legs.

"The kids?" She waved him off. "They aren't a load. They're a joy. I do what I do because I want to, not because I have to."

That was the difference between him and Rainy, he supposed. The responsibilities he resented, she embraced.

Rainy was a better person than him. No surprise there. He had a long way to go to be the man God expected him to be.

"Speaking of kids," she said. "These need to head home. School tomorrow."

He didn't want her to leave.

"Want to do it again sometime? Maybe Friday night?"

Yes, he knew he shouldn't. But he wanted to. No big deal. She was easy to talk to, and they were friends.

Yeah. Friends.

A little voice in his head mocked him. How many other friends had he ever wanted to kiss?

His *friend* tapped him on the chest. His heart somersaulted.

"Do I get to choose the movie next time? Something sappy and romantic. Or maybe sad and maudlin?"

He emitted a groan. "Spare me."

"Don't worry. I won't." She laughed at his grimace, then called toward the living room. "Gather up, gang. Time to roll."

To cover his sudden reluctance to part company, Nate stuck his hands in his back pockets and said, "I'd better walk you out. It's dark out there."

Rainy laughed as he knew she would and huddled close to him. "I'm sooo scared."

Nate grinned, sidelining his sibling woes. Having Rainy cuddled against his side, even as a joke, felt pretty nice—distracting, comfortable, right. To his knowledge, nothing scared this woman. She was a rock, solid in her faith and in the confidence that God had everything under control.

He figured it was true for someone like her. Someone good.

Yawning, the four children gathered their schoolbags and trudged to the van. The dome light glowed like a beacon as they climbed inside.

Nate and Rainy strolled along more slowly, hanging back for a moment alone. Nate had the most conflicted feelings, wanting Rainy near but needing to push her away.

He breathed in the cool April night, the scent of flowers sweet in his lungs. Sweet like Rainy. Out in the pasture, a mama cow mooed low and reassuringly.

Peaceful. Pleasant. He loved this ranch, loved country living.

For a moment, he wondered if a city girl could thrive here. Before the thought could bloom, he nipped it in the bud. Pop and his helpmate talk had put crazy ideas in his head.

In the shadow of the house, Rainy touched his arm. "I really had a good time. Thank you for inviting me. Us."

He stopped there in the darkness, sheltered by the night from prying eyes.

"So are you really going to force a chick flick on me Friday night?"

She grinned. "What do you think?"

He thought he was nuts for asking. Nothing good could come of deepening a relationship with Rainy Jernagen. Nothing at all. One or both of them would end up hurt, and he didn't want that any more than he wanted kids.

But when Rainy beamed that hundred-watt smile at him, he knew he would spend Friday evening with her.

He'd even watch her sappy movie.

Chapter Nine

So this is how it felt to fall in love.

That was the thought running through Rainy's mind as she turned the minivan into her housing addition, coming to a stop behind a yellow school bus. A dozen children emerged, their voices loud as they dispersed, calling to one another and the children remaining on the bus. Familiar sights and sounds to a schoolteacher.

Hands loosely draped over the steering wheel as she waited, Rainy glanced in the rearview mirror. Except for the silly grin on her face, she looked the same.

The difference was on the inside, in a heart so full she wanted to shout with joy. God had sent her four beautiful children to nurture, and now He'd sent Nate into her life to fill the void she hadn't known was there.

Twice today during a parent-teacher conference, her mind had wandered to the cowboy with killer dimples, and she'd lost track of the conversation. Embarrassed, she'd had to say, "Excuse me, will you repeat that?"

As soon as the parents had left, she'd written them a glowing note about their child. Fortunately, the boy was an exceptional student, making the note easy to write. She'd never dreamed falling in love could make her lose her mind. She wasn't some teenybopper with a crush.

No, she was a grown woman with a crush. A serious crush.

The bus rumbled away, and Rainy proceeded to the low-slung house lined with flowers. Her foster children, including two sisters who'd since come and gone, had turned one flower bed into a small vegetable garden. Nate had helped, showing them the proper depth to plant, explaining the need for water and weeding.

He was amazing with the kids. She wondered if he even realized it.

Yesterday Nate had been gone when she'd driven to the ranch to pick up the boys. She had been embarrassingly disappointed.

According to Pop, "Janine hollered frog and Nate jumped."

When he'd phoned later, she'd tried to talk to him about his sister, but he'd changed the subject. Rainy now understood Pop's concerns.

She pulled into the driveway and shut off the engine. As she slid out of the van, dragging a canvas bag of papers to grade, she saw someone out of the corner of her eye.

Turning, she stifled a groan of dismay. For there, in the bright spring sunshine, came Kathy Underkircher. She stormed across Rainy's green patch of grass, her arms swinging at her sides.

Rainy sent a silent prayer heavenward. She needed all the help she could get when confronted by her neighbor.

Kathy, the young grandmother raising her only grandson, lived on a cul-de-sac at the end of the block. Rainy was always amazed that the woman knew everything that went on in the neighborhood, including how many foster children came and went at Rainy's house.

A reasonably attractive woman with dark hair and eyes,

Kathy was stick-skinny and full of nervous energy. To Rainy's knowledge, she had no outside job. As a result, she stuck her nose into every area of the neighborhood. As president of the neighborhood housing authority, a voluntary position that Kathy seemed to relish so much she'd been seen measuring the length of someone's grass with a ruler, she often threatened to cite neighbors for the slightest infraction. Recently, she'd protested the vegetable garden, calling the tiny plot unauthorized.

Before Rainy could say hello, Kathy had her nose pressed against the van windows, peering inside with her usual scowl. "What have you done with those children?"

Though tempted to say they were locked in the cellar without food and water, where all children belonged, Rainy bit back the smart reply. No use antagonizing an antagonistic woman.

"The girls are at Brownies. The boys are working on their fair project." Determined to be a Christian no matter what, Rainy kept her face and tone pleasant. "How are you, Kathy? Today is a gorgeous day, isn't it?"

For indeed it was. Windless, a rarity in Oklahoma, with bright sunshine and a sky so blue she could almost taste it. Across the street, Sara Bishop pushed a red lawnmower, filling the air with the fresh spring scent of newly cut grass.

Kathy wasn't interested. Her nose quivered with indignation. "I've seen that man over here."

Rainy's stomach tightened. So much for niceties. "What man?"

"That cowboy in the big pickup truck. Making all the racket, noise pollution. Don't think you're fooling anyone, Miss Jernagen."

Rainy blinked, trying to follow. "I'm afraid you've lost me, Ms. Underkircher."

The woman's lips tightened smugly. "Play coy all you want. The DHS knows what I'm talking about."

Hair prickled at the back of Rainy's neck. She could deal with the woman's dislike, but an all-out character attack was a different matter. "Kathy, if you have something to say, say it. I know you're the person calling the police and social services."

"Someone has to look after the welfare of innocent children."

Emotion boiled up. Frustration, anxiety, outrage. Rainy tightened her grip on the schoolbag. The rough canvas bit into her fingertips.

"Let me assure you of this. I take care of my children. I love them. They're happy here."

Kathy tossed her head and sniffed. "I hear their screams of terror. No telling what you're doing to them. Children belong with their real mother, not some high and mighty school teacher."

Rainy shut her eyes briefly, counted to three, and tried again. "I've explained Katie's problems to you. The social worker has explained them, as well. I'm sure you've noticed that Katie is making improvements." She adjusted the shoulder bag, which seemed to grow heavier with each unpleasant moment. "Please, can't you and I resolve the problem between us and leave the children out of it?"

"You'd like that, wouldn't you? You'd like for me to go away and let you go on mistreating children the way you mistreated my Conrad." Her face contorted in dislike. "Other people may think you're a saint because you take in foster children, but I know the truth."

Any conversation always came back to her grandson. "I'm very sorry if I caused you or Conrad any embarrassment, Ms. Underkircher. Truly."

She didn't know what else to do to resolve the issue. She wasn't going to apologize for doing her job properly, and she had no power over stories printed by the local newspaper.

Kathy ignored the effort at conciliation. She leaned forward, her green eyes as glittering and hard as cut glass. "Who is that man? I saw his truck here late Tuesday night and again the next morning. I told the DHS. We don't need that kind of thing in our neighborhood. What would the real mothers of these kids think if they knew what their children were being exposed to?"

Rainy squelched the urge to roll her eyes. The birth mothers of these children were the reason she was a foster mom. These kids had experienced plenty of horrors before being placed with her.

She also remembered the reason Nate had come to her house Tuesday night and again the next morning. At her call, he had hurried over to fix a leak under the kitchen sink but didn't have the correct size pipe. After turning the water off for the night, he'd returned early the next morning to complete the repair.

But there was no use explaining the innocent situation to Kathy. She didn't want the truth. She wanted some sort of revenge. All the talking and explaining in the world would not satisfy her.

Giving up, Rainy said, "I really need to go, Ms. Underkircher. You'll have to excuse me."

Hiking up the canvas tote, she started up the walk to her porch. Kathy's voice followed her. "You won't be so smart when they take those children away for good and you lose all that money you're making off someone else's misfortune."

Rainy didn't look back, but Kathy had finally hit a nerve. Her back teeth clenched as anger boiled in her belly. She didn't take in foster children for the money. Every penny went to the children's needs. If she had her way and could adopt them, she'd receive nothing at all. And that was fine. *Fine.* Because she loved *them,* not the measly little checks they brought with them.

Inside the house, she dropped her keys and bag on the

coffee table and slumped onto the couch. Her head in her hands, she took deep breaths and tried to calm down. Her jaws ached with tension as the familiar worry crept in. What would happen if social services believed Kathy's accusations? Would she lose the children?

Scriptures floated through her head—about not giving into anger, about loving her enemies, about trusting God with everything. Only last week she'd presented a puppet skit for Children's Church about getting along with difficult friends. With a self-deprecating huff, she thought maybe her puppets could teach her a thing or two.

Her doorbell sounded, a regular *ding-dong* since Nate had dismantled the hard rock music. She stiffened. If Kathy was back, Rainy wasn't sure what she might do.

Cautiously, she peered out, saw Sara Bishop from across the street and opened the door.

"Hi, Sara," she said, enormously relieved. "Come on in."

Sara, her face shiny with perspiration from yard work, shook her head. "No, thanks. I just wanted to make sure you're okay."

"You heard what Kathy said," Rainy said, chagrined.

"Everyone in the neighborhood hears her opinions on a regular basis." Sara pushed at damp bangs. Her brown hair stuck straight up in front. "Kathy's a loose cannon, Rainy, a pitiful woman with nothing to do but make others miserable. I know you take good care of the children who come here. I wanted you to know most people don't share her opinion."

Grateful, Rainy touched the other woman's arm. Sara's skin was hot and damp. "Thank you, Sara. That means a lot to me. I keep worrying that she'll complain so much the authorities will start to believe her. Where there's smoke there's fire and all that." She opened the door wider. "Are you sure you won't come in? I was about to make some tea."

"No, no. We have a baseball game tonight. I want to finish cutting the grass before Rodney gets home from work."

"And before Kathy cites you with failure to keep a tidy lawn."

They both chuckled. "Exactly. Better mow yours, too. It's over an inch and a half. Kathy will be over here with her ruler."

Though amusing, there was truth in the warning. "I'll have Will start on it tonight."

"Then she'll protest on the grounds of child labor laws." Sara laughed and stepped off the porch.

With a wave, she recrossed the street and cranked the lawnmower. At the burst of sound, flecks of grass whirl-winded around Sara's green-stained tennis shoes. Rainy stood in the door watching, thankful for a thoughtful neighbor.

But Kathy's visit had put a damper on her joy. It had also reminded her that Will, Joshua, Emma and Katie were not her children. Not yet. If anything went wrong, they might never be.

"Something bothering you?" Nate cut the wire on a bale of hay and kicked the alfalfa with the toe of his boot, scattering chunks around for the horses. Three equine heads dipped to munch. Rainy had arrived with Emma and Katie a good thirty minutes ago and hadn't said a dozen words. "You're kind of quiet."

Normally, she talked his ears off, telling him about things that happened at school, a new puppet show idea, enthusing over his cows, his horses, his ranch. He looked forward to her chatter, if he was honest. The ranch seemed quiet, dull, even lifeless until she arrived.

He didn't understand why, but he simply felt better when she was here. Today something was wrong. He was certain.

"Come on, Slick, talk to Papa," he said, shooting her a grin intended to make her smile in return. "What's up?"

Absently, she ran her hand over the glossy bent neck of a bay horse. With an uncharacteristically heavy sigh, she told him about a confrontation with her neighbor, finishing with, "I've done everything I know to get on that woman's good side, and I've failed."

Nate gathered up several pieces of baling wire and rolled them into a loop. "Maybe she doesn't have a good side."

"I'm starting to think you're right. My mother keeps telling me to kill her with kindness, go the extra mile, etc., but I don't know what else to do. I've talked to her, sent her cards, baked her brownies—"

Nate held up a hand. "If the brownies didn't do it, she's hopeless."

That got a smile out of her. She climbed up on the metal fence and perched, a pair of yellow slip-on shoes hanging off the backs of her feet. "What if she jeopardizes my foster-mom status?"

Nate tossed the looped wire into a barrel. At the rattle, a fat crow perched on the eave of the shed squawked and flapped away. Nate glanced toward Emma and Katie, hanging upside down in the tire swing he and Pop had erected in a backyard oak.

"Can she do that?"

"Being single is already a strike against me. If she convinces social services that I'm doing something wrong…" Her voice trailed off. She bit her bottom lip.

Nate's protective hackles rose. Even though he wished she'd let someone else do the job, Nate didn't like the idea of anyone criticizing Rainy. She was amazing. Awesome. Real cute, too.

"You're a great foster mom. They're lucky to have you."

Though he could never do what she did, he also couldn't imagine Rainy without children around her. She was made to be a mother. In fact, he couldn't figure out why she wasn't married with a houseful of her own kids. Some guy was really missing out.

His protective urge turned green at the thought of Rainy with someone else. He had no right to feel possessive or protective, but he did.

He'd have to work on that, but right now Rainy needed his support. If he was a tad too happy about that piece of knowledge, he'd have to work on that, too. Later.

"What can I do to help?" Hadn't she asked him the same thing once?

Shaking her head, she banged the heel of her shoe against the metal railing in a steady, clanging rhythm. "Nothing, I'm afraid. She's seen your truck at my house. She thinks you and I have something illicit going on."

At the outrageous accusation, Nate bristled. "You can't be serious."

Rainy banged her shoe again and it fell off, tumbling to the dirt. "I wish I wasn't."

Nate retrieved the fallen shoe and caught her by the heel. "Here you go, Cinderella. You've lost your slipper."

He slid the shoe onto her foot but didn't release his hold. Sitting above him, Rainy leaned forward, placed her hands on his shoulders and smiled. For the first time since she'd arrived, the smile was happy.

Something warm and full pressed inside Nate's chest. He wanted Rainy to be happy—always.

"I guess that makes you my Prince Charming," she said.

Prince Charming? Him? Not even close.

"Come on, I'll help you down. I have a surprise."

"You rented another chick flick?" she asked, a twinkle in her eyes.

He made a rude noise, thrilled when she responded with a fullblown laugh. Now they were getting somewhere.

Bracketing her narrow waist with his hands, he lifted her

down. "Remember when Emma and Katie said they wanted a calf to take care of, too?"

"You didn't get them a calf, did you?" She grabbed his arm. "Nate, they're too little for that."

He patted her hand where she grasped his upper arm in a death grip. "Don't freak out until you see. I'll show you first and if you think it's okay, we'll show the girls. Deal?"

She looked dubious but followed him toward his surprise. He'd planned to wait a few days to give the gift, but Rainy needed the distraction today.

He opened the wooden door to a small storage shed he'd cleaned out this morning, keeping himself between Rainy and the animal inside. "I'm keeping him in here for now while he's so young."

She tiptoed up on her silly, impractical shoes, trying to see over him. Nate was too tall and wide for that. "Are you going to show me or not?"

"Tsk, tsk. So impatient."

Widening her eyes in joking defiance, she spun away as if to leave. He caught her arm, laughing softly, uncommonly happy, as he turned her back around and led the way into the dimly lit building.

A small bleat came from the corner. Rainy looked at him in question, but before he could say a word, a snow-white baby goat tottered into view. The little critter came toward him, bleating away, recognizing him as the meal giver. Nate touched the warm, woolly head with affection.

Suddenly, it was very important for Rainy to like his surprise. "Baby goats are supposed to make good pets. I thought Emma and Katie would like him. He's real gentle. A nice little fella. He won't get very big. What do you think?"

"Oh, Nate. He's perfect. *Perfect!*" Rainy threw her arms around him and hugged, knocking him backward several steps. "You are the most thoughtful, incredible, kindest man in the universe."

What else could he do? As he stumbled back to catch his balance, he took Rainy with him, wrapped her up like a present and held her close. Her coconut scent swirled around him in a cloud of pleasure, mixing with the scent of dust. What man could resist a woman who thought he was all that?

Other than the tiny goat nudging at his pants leg, he and Rainy were alone. One of those rare moments. Rainy gazed up at him. He gazed down at her, into eyes so full of light and love that he paid no attention to his previous reservations. He bowed his head and kissed her.

Rainy didn't take kissing lightly. In fact, she could count the number of guys she'd kissed on one hand. All those other times had been awkward and a little embarrassing.

Sharing a kiss with Nate was as natural as breathing. Only better. Everything in her wanted to burst out with the news that she loved him. But she didn't. Not yet.

"I've been wanting to do that for a while," he said, holding her lightly around the waist, his head bent so they were eye to eye, the tip of his hat shading them. His breath was warm and pleasant against her skin, the scent of him redolent of hay and leather.

"I've been wanting you to," Rainy admitted, not at all surprised when the words came out a little shaky. She rested her hands on his shirtfront, felt the smooth cotton and hard buttons against her fingertips.

She would always remember every detail of that kiss, she thought. Here in the small, dim shed, straw and dirt beneath her feet, the baby goat bleating, dust motes floating in the perforated sunbeams.

Nothing at all romantic about the setting, but Rainy considered it perfect.

Nate's supple mouth curved upward. "Want to do it again?"

"We have an audience."

"That old goat?" he teased, smiling wide, dimples deep, when she laughed at his clever reference to the new pet. "He won't mind."

Rainy tiptoed up and touched her mouth to his, a quick, light kiss before stepping away. "There you go."

He brought her fingers up and brushed them with his lips. Rainy nearly melted.

Forcing a lighter voice than she felt, she said, "Let's go tell the girls about their new friend. They're going to love him."

Two beats passed while Nate stared into her face. Then with a wink, he tugged her toward the door. "Whatever your heart desires."

That part was easy. Her heart desired him and the beautiful relationship growing between them.

They'd turned a corner today. For Rainy there was no going back.

Chapter Ten

Rainy's fingers shook with excitement as she held the day's mail in one hand and, with the other, jiggled the key in the front door. A gentle rain fell, washing the street in shades of dark and light, but even rain could not dampen Rainy's spirits. She'd been waiting a long time for the official-looking envelope from social services telling her she could begin the proceedings to adopt Katie. In another year, she hoped to do the same for the other three children.

"Katie, you and Emma change into play clothes while I read the mail." For once, she didn't have half a dozen things to do after school. Other than the regular evening trip to Crossroads Ranch, which was more of a treat than a task, she could relax for a few minutes.

"Can we have a snack?" Emma asked.

"Change first. Then you can each have some fruit and milk. Deal?"

"Then can we go play with Snowflake?"

"Sure," she said, smiling as Emma skipped happily down the hall with Katie right behind.

Emma and Katie had gone wild with excitement the day Nate had presented them with the goat, whom they'd quickly dubbed Snowflake. They'd danced around the pen stirring up dust and singing, "Nate, Nate, Nate is great" until Will had given both a quarter to stop.

Each day since, they looked forward to the trip to the ranch with exuberant delight, frequently taking along their own version of grooming tools—Rainy's old hair curlers. Barrettes, ribbons. Snowflake didn't seem to mind at all that he'd become their beauty parlor model.

Rainy looked forward to the daily outing, as well. But her enthusiasm had nothing to do with the animals and everything to do with the cowboy. Many evenings, unless school or church activities required their attendance, she and the kids stayed at Crossroads until dark. When other functions beckoned, Nate had taken to coming along.

Rainy thrilled with the belief that she meant as much to Nate as he meant to her.

Only last night, she'd sat next to him at a basketball game, yelling her throat raw for the Summervale Sonics. He'd taken into stride Emma hanging over his back and Joshua pestering him with questions about the game.

There had been an uncomfortable moment when Guy Bartlett had spotted her and climbed the bleachers to say hello. When he'd realized she was with Nate he'd behaved oddly. So had Nate. They'd reminded her of a couple of bristle-haired dogs, eyeing each other with polite suspicion.

Guy had become increasingly pushy lately, not wanting to take no for an answer, though he'd never bother to ask if she was seeing anyone. As if no one else could possibly be interested. He was a decent man, one she disliked hurting, but hopefully he'd gotten the message.

After Guy departed, Nate had been different, protective, acting almost possessive.

Then, at one point when the Sonics fired a go-ahead three pointer, they'd erupted upward with the crowd to high-five each other. When they settled back onto the hard bench, Nate pulled her hand against his knee…and kept it there.

A family. They felt like a family.

And family was the reason for her excitement today.

Rainy ripped the thick envelope open, quickly scanned the letter before waving the papers at the ceiling and crying a delighted, "Thank you, Lord!"

Too excited to keep the news to herself, she grabbed the telephone and dialed, hoping, hoping Nate was in the house and not out in the pasture somewhere.

"Crossroads Ranch."

"Hey, Cowboy. Are you busy?"

"You sound…different. Is everything okay?"

"Everything is perfect. I'm so happy. I needed someone to share my good news."

A soft chuckle. "Share away. The bus hasn't gotten here with the boys yet, so I came in for a cold drink."

Rainy settled on her kid-friendly, fake leather sofa and curled her feet beneath her. "My adoption paperwork is in process. Pending court approval and if nothing goes haywire, I'll be officially Mom to Katie by the time school resumes in the fall."

A momentary silence hummed through the lines.

"Nate? Did we get cut off?"

"I'm here. That's great, Rainy." Was that hesitation in his voice?

An odd prickle of doubt teased the back of Rainy's mind. She tamped the worry down.

"I need to celebrate. Want to come over after the boys do their chores? I could order pizza. Bake some brownies."

Again that strange silence. "Sorry. Can't make it."

"Oh." Talk about deflating her joy balloon.

Then as if he knew he'd disappointed her, he said, "Something's come up. My sister called."

His sister. Again. Her disappointment turned to annoyance. "Nate, did you ever think of telling her no?"

"I can't."

"That's absurd. Of course you can. Unless she's truly having an emergency, dial her number and tell her you have something else to do."

His heavy sigh seemed magnified through the telephone. "I can't do that."

"Why not? Why do you let them run your life?"

"I'd much rather…" He blew out another breath, frustrated, trapped between his siblings and the woman he wanted to be with. Worse yet, Rainy had sprung the adoption thing on him, tying him into more knots.

"What is it, Nate? Talk to me."

He could do that much. He owed her that much. "When we were kids, Janine was injured in an accident. It was my fault. I owe her."

Nate didn't want to go into the ugly details. And he sure wasn't going to tell her about Christine, but she deserved to know why he was obligated to care for his siblings no matter the cost to his personal life.

"I was driving a tractor on my mother's family farm. Janine ran in front me. I hit her."

He shuddered at the memory of his four-year-old sister falling beneath the wheel of the tractor. "Broke her legs, crushed her pelvis. No one even knew if she'd survive."

"I'm sorry, Nate. That's awful." Her tone, annoyed before, had gone quietly horrified. "How old were you?"

"Nine."

"Nine! What was a nine-year-old doing driving a tractor?"

"My dad wasn't around much, so, as the oldest, his share of the work fell to me. It's a fact of farm life. Everyone works."

"I'm sorry for what happened. Truly I am, Nate, but you

can't blame yourself for an accident that occurred when you were Joshua's age. Think about it. Would you let Joshua drive a tractor?"

"Of course not," he said. "He didn't grow up on a farm. I did." Joshua hadn't caused a sister's death, either. But Nate had.

"You need to let it go."

"I expected you to understand," he said, though his bitterness was not directed against Rainy.

He was trapped in this miserable situation with his brother and sister. He wanted things to be different, but they never would be. They were his siblings and therefore his responsibility.

"Nate?" Rainy spoke through the line, softly pleading. "I'm sorry. Your relationship with your brother and sister is none of my business. I should never have said anything."

Now he really felt like a jerk. She'd been excited when she first called, wanting him to share in her celebration. Instead of being there for her, he'd turned the conversation around to his own selfish concerns.

Proof positive that he'd been right all along. Nate Del Rio did not have what it took to make anyone happy. Not even himself.

The next afternoon, all four children in tow because of counseling appointments, Rainy arrived home to find a vase full of red roses on her porch.

"Bet they're from Nate," Will said, giving his glasses a shove for good measure.

"We don't bet," Rainy said automatically, though knowing Will's word choice was only a figure of speech.

"Well, if we did, I'd win." Will grinned an ornery grin and stuck his thumbs in his back pockets the way Nate often did.

Rainy thought his imitation of the cowboy was adorable.

She'd begun to see other similarities between the man and the boy, as well. Will had never known a consistent father, and to her way of thinking, he had chosen a good man to imitate.

She slid the tiny envelope from its forked, plastic holder and took out the card, praying they weren't from Guy. She hadn't heard from him since the ballgame. Though sad to lose his friendship, enough was enough. Nate's signature was scrawled across the card with a message.

"Yes," she said to Will. "You'd win."

The children pressed in around her. "What does it say? Is it all lovey-dovey?"

"Joshua!" she said, turning surprised eyes on the nine-year-old.

"We're not babies, Rainy. We know he likes you."

Her heart skipped a beat. "I like him, too."

"Are you going to get married?" Will gnawed the corner of his lip and shifted his black backpack from his shoulders to the porch step. Did he like the idea? Or was he worried about it?

Before Rainy could think how best to answer, Katie lifted her face from sniffing the roses and said, "I never had a daddy. Can Nate be my daddy now?"

"Kids, hold on. Nate sent roses, not a wedding ring."

"First comes love, then comes marriage," Joshua said matter-of-factly.

"I haven't even read the card. He may say he's running off to Tahiti with a hula girl." She handed her keys to Will. "Unlock the door and let's go inside before the entire neighborhood knows our business."

Particularly Kathy Underkircher.

"Where's Tahiti?" Emma asked. "Is it close to Tulsa?"

Her heart light, Rainy laughed and followed the children inside, the spray of roses filling her head with their soft scent, the way a certain cowboy filled her heart with joy. She set the vase on the kitchen table and turned the card over to read.

"Congratulations on your good news. You're an amazing mother. Sorry I rained on your parade. Love, Nate."

Love. He'd written *love*. Did he mean it, or did he use the word casually, as so many people did today? Either way, Rainy was thrilled. He'd sent her roses and an apology.

Maybe she'd been too hard on him last night about his siblings. As the oldest brother, with no parents left to help, he felt obligated. One of the things she admired about Nate was his strong sense of responsibility and care for other people. Wasn't that why he'd joined the Handyman Ministry? Wasn't that what helped make him a successful rancher and a committed Christian?

"Miss Rainy, there's something on the back of the card, too."

Emma stood at her elbow staring up at the card in Rainy's hand, her pretty blonde head tilted back.

Rainy flipped the card over and laughed. "Pizza is on the way. So am I. Please bake brownies."

Maybe he could do this. Maybe he could make this work.

With three pizza boxes stacked on one arm and the hot Italian smell filling his nostrils, Nate stood on Rainy's porch. The roses he'd left earlier had disappeared and he smiled a little to himself, thinking of her reaction. He hoped she wasn't allergic or anything.

Inside the house, Katie's high-pitched scream rattled the windows. According to Rainy, the little redhead was down to about two screams a day, a big drop from every few minutes.

Rainy was a wonder woman with those kids.

A knot formed in his belly as the dilemma presented itself

again and again. Falling for Rainy meant accepting these
foster children. No, not accepting. Loving. Rainy was a love-
me-love-my-kids kind of woman. Even if they weren't officially her kids.

Nate still didn't know if he could do that. He cared for
Rainy. He liked being with her. Looked forward to that
moment each day when her car came flying down the long
drive to Crossroads Ranch, spewing dust and gravel in her
rush to arrive.

Anyway, he liked to think she was rushing to be with him.
Fool that he was.

They'd never actually discussed his feelings about kids,
though nothing had changed his mind about not having any
of his own. He liked her four munchkins. They'd grown on
him. But he worried about them, too. He didn't like that part.

Now he was trapped into spending time with them. Sort
of. Rainy with her pushy sweetness had shoved her way into
his life and onto his ranch, bringing the kids along. Now they
all had projects, reasons to be there every single day. When
he wasn't scared out of his mind with worry, he enjoyed
them.

He jabbed the doorbell again, concerned that no one had
ripped the door open yet. Hadn't she read the card?

Truth was, he'd stopped minding about the kids' projects
long ago. They gave him an excuse to see Rainy on a daily basis.

So the problem was exacerbated. He'd been praying a lot
about what to do. Should he break things off before he got
in too deep? Or was he already too late?

Before he could answer his own questions, Rainy opened
the door, smiled her sweet smile and invited him into the celebration.

An hour later, the celebration turned to despair.

Rainy had just slid a pan of brownies into the oven. All

four kids had chocolate batter somewhere on their happy faces. Her cowboy was leaning on the blue Formica, looking so handsome her heart was about to burst with happiness, when the doorbell rang.

"Grand Central," she said, grinning at Nate. Her doorbell rang often, usually neighborhood children coming over to play.

Surrounded by the kids, she opened the door. The social worker, briefcase hanging at her side, stood on the porch.

"Mrs. Chadwick, you're working late tonight."

"I'm sorry to bother you, Rainy," she said. "May I come in? We need to talk."

Something about the way the social worker said the words warned Rainy that this was not a casual visit. Rainy let her in, motioning her to the couch.

All four children, wide-eyed as always when anyone of authority appeared, started to slither away. Nate appeared in the archway between the dining and living rooms. The children reoriented, moving to his side like iron filings to a magnet. In a flash of understanding, Rainy realized the kids felt safe with Nate by their sides.

Rainy made the introductions. Mrs. Chadwick, her smile a little weary, said to Nate, "Oh, so you're the cowboy in the big pickup truck."

Rainy and Nate looked at each other. "Mrs. Underkircher," they said at the same time.

Mrs. Chadwick raised and lowered her eyebrows. "Yes."

"Is that why you're here so late?" Rainy asked. "Is something wrong? More complaints?"

Mrs. Chadwick glanced at Nate who took the hint.

"Should I leave?" he asked.

"That's up to Rainy." The woman placed her valise on the couch next to her and clicked it open. "The children, on the other hand, don't need to be present."

Rainy's stomach dropped. This didn't sound good at all.

Will pushed away from the pack, his skinny bird chest heaving. He stopped in front of the social worker, fists tight, chin up, eyes blazing behind the brown glasses. "You're not taking us away. We won't go."

Nate dropped a hand onto Will's thin shoulder. "Easy, buddy."

"No one's going anywhere today, Will," the woman assured him. "However, I need to talk to Miss Rainy in private, okay?"

No one was going anywhere *today*. At Mrs. Chadwick's carefully chosen words, cold fear trickled like ice water down Rainy's spine.

Please, Lord, she prayed silently. *Please don't let that be the reason for her visit*.

Nate, bless him, must have seen the panic rising in Rainy's face.

"The kids and I will go out back and shoot baskets or something," he told her, his gaze lingering for a long moment as if concerned about leaving her alone. Rainy desperately wanted him to stay, needing his support in a way she'd never expected to. His idea was better, though. The children needed him most of all.

"I'd appreciate that, Nate. Thanks."

"No problem. Holler if you need me." He gave the social worker a warning glance, then said to the kids with feigned joviality, "How about it, gang? Want to play a game of horse with a worn-out old cowboy?"

The children cast worried glances at the social worker and Rainy, but allowed Nate to shuffle them out the back door.

Though equally anxious about the unexpected visit from the social worker, Rainy's heart squeezed with gratitude that Nate would do this. The last time he'd played basketball with the children, he'd let Emma and Katie sit on his shoulders to shoot the ball. They'd loved every minute of it. So had she.

"He's very protective," Mrs. Chadwick said with a wry smile as soon as the back door clicked shut.

"He's a good friend. The kids adore him."

"Is he the one letting the boys raise a calf on his ranch?"

"Now the girls have a baby goat," Rainy said, eager to dispel any ugly rumors Kathy Underkircher may have started. "All four children are learning responsibility out there, taking care of animals, learning to ride a horse, observing good male role models. Nate and his grandfather have been good for the children."

The social worker held up a hand to stop Rainy's flow of words. "I'm not the one you have to convince, Rainy. You're one of the best foster parents we have."

"Sorry. I guess I'm worried that my neighbor will paint me with such a dark brush you'll start believing her. Or that something will go wrong with the children's adoptions."

The other woman looped a lock of short hair behind one ear and avoided Rainy's eyes. Tired rings circled her eyes. Rainy knew for a fact her caseload was enormous, working her long hours.

"That's why I'm here. Something *has* gone wrong."

Rainy felt the earth shift. "But it can't have. I received an official letter about Katie yesterday."

The social worker's reply was gentle and compassionate. "So did Katie's birth mother."

A sick feeling began to churn in Rainy's stomach. "I thought she was in prison."

"She was. She's been released. When she received the letter, as was her right, she apparently became extremely upset and contacted a lawyer." Mrs. Chadwick handed Rainy a document from the valise. "She has filed to regain custody."

Rainy stared at the piece of paper as if it were a rattle-snake. As she quickly read through the official document, the bottom dropped out of her life. "She can't do this. They won't let her. Not after what she let happen to Katie—"

The social worker placed a hand on her arm. "I know, Rainy. I know. But legally, she has a right to protest the adoption."

"Can she take Katie away?" Rainy rubbed her throat, tight with emotion, determined to hold back the threatening tears.

"I won't lie to you. If the courts believe she has been re-habilitated and can give Katie a stable home, then she will likely regain custody."

"I've had Katie for so long. She's my little girl."

"Rainy, you've known from the beginning that this could happen. All of these children, not just Katie, are legal risk adoptions."

Rainy slowly shook her head from side to side, sick and shaking. A sour taste rose in the back of her throat. "I can't let her go, knowing what happened to her before. I can't."

"Then I suggest you contact a lawyer." Mrs. Chadwick closed her valise and stood to leave. "Remember, Rainy, I'm on your side. I will testify on your behalf. But if things don't work out, there are plenty of other children who need what you have to offer."

With that painfully true statement, the woman took her leave, shutting the door behind her. Rainy sat on the couch, her insides trembling. Yes, there were plenty of needy children, but she loved Katie. And she feared for her little girl's safety.

For several minutes, Rainy sat frozen, unable to think, unable to react. She was vaguely aware of cars passing by outside, of the smell of baked brownies, of how cold her sock-clad feet had grown. Almost as cold as her insides. She shivered.

How in the world could she tell Katie? Or any of the children, for that matter. They'd be terrified that they were next. And what if they were?

Oh, Lord, oh, Lord, give me courage and strength and wisdom.

The back door banged open. Nate and the children came in without their usual exuberance. They must have seen Mrs. Chadwick's car pull away.

Nate took one look at Rainy and sank down beside her, taking her cold hand in his. "Hey, you okay?"

She shook her head and, in a whisper, answered, "No. Very bad news."

"Want to talk about it?"

She nodded, fighting back tears, not wanting to fall apart, but fearing she might. "Yes, but not in front of the kids."

"Miss Rainy." Will stood in the entry between the kitchen and the living room, his face anxious, twisting his hands. "I smell something burning."

"Oh my goodness, the brownies!" Rainy leaped up and rushed into the kitchen, yanked the scorched dessert from the oven with a potholder. This was too much. Too hard. She couldn't bear it. "I've burned them. They're ruined."

She burst into tears.

"Hey now. Hey." Nate took her by the shoulders, his voice stunned, maybe even scared. "Don't cry."

She knew the tears were not for the lost brownies, but the children wouldn't know that. She couldn't let them know. At least not yet. Not until she'd spoken with an attorney.

Oh, Lord, oh, Lord. The silent cry for help rolled over and over in her head.

She covered her face, her body quaking as she tried to regain composure. Without a word, Nate pulled her into his arms, one strong hand stroking her hair over and over again. His silence told her that he understood.

Rainy felt the presence of the children, felt their concern, their worry. They'd never seen her cry before.

"It's okay, Miss Rainy," Joshua said, patting her back with his small, warm hand. "I like burned brownies. We all like burned brownies. Okay? Don't cry. We'll eat every single one of them."

The child's desperate attempt to encourage and comfort touched Rainy to the soul. She cried all the harder. Bless his precious, tender heart. Regardless of his personal trauma, he never liked seeing anyone sad or upset. For his sake, if for no other reason, she had to pull herself together.

Rainy drew in a quivering *hu-hu-hu,* and looked over Nate's shoulder to the boy's worried face. On a shudder, she sniffed and said, "Oh, Joshy, I love you."

Blinking back new tears, she managed a watery smile. The children, disturbed to see the usually upbeat Rainy cry over a pan of brownies, hovered around, patting and consoling. Will broke away and went to the counter to gaze at the steaming pan. Without a word, he took down a plate, got out a spatula, and set to work.

"They're still good," he said, adjusting his glasses. "Just a little toasted on the bottom. We can scrape that off. They'll be delicious."

"I love toasted brownies," Katie said, catching the spirit from Joshua and Will. She rubbed her tummy. "Yum."

Emma looked from Katie to her brothers and then to Rainy, expression puzzled. When Joshua nudged her, she blinked a few times. Then with false exuberance, she said, "Me, too. With milk. Lots of milk."

Her reaction was so cute Rainy chuckled. Seeing his chance, Nate jumped in, too.

"Sounds great to me. Toasted brownies and lots of milk."

Keeping one hand on Rainy's shoulder as though he expected her to topple onto the beige vinyl flooring at any moment, he slowly stepped away, reached for a paper towel and began to pat the tears from her cheeks. Rainy caught the towel and gently took over. She was feeling embarrassed enough without having Nate dry her tears.

Although the gesture was awfully sweet.

"I'm okay now," she said. "Thank you, all of you, for being so nice, but we don't need to eat burned brownies. I can make more."

"Oh, no, you don't." Nate's lips twitched with humor. "Neither rain nor snow nor tears nor laughter will stop us from eating those brownies now."

"Nate," she said, with one final sniff and shiver. Her face felt swollen and distorted.

He pointed at her. "No argument."

So with a heavy heart bolstered by the love and compassion of four children and a cowboy, Rainy pulled up a chair and ate her share of slightly scorched, crispy-edged brownies.

The moment tasted absolutely delicious.

Chapter Eleven

Nate's guts were in a knot. This was exactly why he never wanted kids. Trouble. Heartache. Tears.

When the children eventually scattered to do homework and take baths, Rainy had told him the bad news. So, while putting on a happy face along with Rainy, he'd stayed until the children were tucked in bed and had fought down his own furious reaction while he read a bedtime story to a quartet of soap-scented, pajama-clad children. He'd never read a bedtime story before, and the emotion clogging his throat would have choked a horse. A Clydesdale.

"Surely the court will see what a great home you've given Katie and how much she's blossomed here," he told Rainy after the two of them had returned to the living room alone.

With the children in bed, the house had grown oddly silent. Silent, and still smelling of scorched chocolate. Which wasn't half bad, come to think of it. He would have eaten charcoal if he'd had to. Anything to see Rainy smile again.

"I can only hope," Rainy said. "Now I understand how a parent could take her child and run away during a custody battle."

"You wouldn't do that, would you?"

Rainy shook her head. "Running would only make things worse. Besides, I have the other children to consider. I'm scared, Nate. Scared of losing her. Scared of letting her go back to a life that hurt her."

Rainy had told him previously about the abuse Katie had suffered at the hands of her birth mother's boyfriend. He could understand her concern. The Neanderthal in him wanted to meet the guy in an alley somewhere and teach him a lesson. Little Katie was a screamer, but she was a doll face, too. She had taken a while to warm up to him, to trust that he wouldn't hurt her, but now the cute redhead dogged his footsteps, presented him with wildflowers and roly-poly bugs, and teased him by running away with his hat.

"Do you have an attorney?" he asked.

She shook her head. "No. I think there are a couple in the church, though."

"That's a good start. Want me to call Pastor Jim for a recommendation?"

"I'll do it." She sucked her bottom lip between her teeth and gnawed.

Nate was particularly fond of that lip and to see it gnawed in stress didn't set well. "Don't give up. We'll fight."

"Lawyers are expensive. The cost of a court battle will be enormous." Wearily, she pushed both hands into the sides of hair. "I'll get the money. I just don't know where."

"Do you have any savings?"

"Not much. Most of it was spent on Katie's private counseling."

"I thought the department of human services paid for that kind of thing."

"I wanted her to have the best in Christian counseling, and the system wouldn't pay for faith-based sessions. Dr. Baker has helped her more than anyone, so I don't regret one penny." She spread her hands wide, managing a sad smile. "But it's left me a little short of ready cash."

Nate's heart turned over. Acid indigestion, maybe from burned brownies, maybe from another source entirely, burned in his belly.

"I might be able to get a loan or take a second mortgage on my house. I don't know." Her lip quivered, just about doing Nate in for good. He'd never seen her cry until tonight. Never seen her anything but optimistic and peppy. If she cried again, he might have to do something drastic.

"Don't borrow trouble. Talk to a lawyer first. See where you stand. We'll get the money."

Her face brightened. "What's this *we* stuff?"

He was wondering the same thing. All he knew for sure was that he wouldn't let her fight this alone.

Three days later, Nate put the finishing touches on a boot shine as Pop ambled in from the garage, wiping his grease-covered hands on a red rag.

"Where you headed, Nate boy?"

"Town." He stashed the shoe polish beneath the sink. "Need anything?"

"Might pick up some oil for the hay truck, and maybe a box of those gummy fruit doo-dads."

"Gummy fruits? Since when did you start eating gummy fruits?"

"Ah, not for me," Pop said. "The kids is fond of them, especially that Emma."

Nate hid a grin. "Got you wrapped around her little finger, doesn't she?"

"No more than you are."

He jerked a shoulder. "You know how I feel about kids."

"Yep, probably better than you do. I also know how you

feel about Miss Rainy." Pop opened the refrigerator and took out a pitcher of cold water.

Nate made a slow turn toward his grandfather. "Yeah? Well, I wish you'd share this great wisdom with me, because I sure don't."

Pitcher in hand, Pop stared long and hard until Nate glanced away. There was something going on inside his grandfather's head and to tell the truth, Nate didn't want to hear it. He didn't know what to do about Rainy. He didn't even know how he felt about her.

Fortunately for him, Pop let the topic go in favor of more pressing concerns. "Any progress on the custody hearing?"

Nate had told Pop the story, including Rainy's cash-flow problem. He hadn't, however, told his grandfather that he'd come up with a solution.

He sucked in a deep breath. The smell and flavor of fried bacon still hung in the air from the BLT they'd had for lunch. "She was turned down for a second mortgage."

"What a shame." Pop splashed milk into a glass. "Don't seem right that a woman trying to protect a child ought to be in this situation."

Nate felt the same way. In fact, he'd wrestled with the idea since the moment Rainy had called him, stressed over the star-tling sum of money required to retain a lawyer and to fight a custody battle. Last night, he'd prayed for hours and then had awakened long before daybreak to pray again. He knew what he had to do. What he *wanted* to do. No matter how much it hurt.

"I'm going to give her the money."

Pop lowered the drinking glass from his lips and slowly slid into a straight-backed chair. "Where do you plan to come up with that much cash?"

Nate went to the kitchen window and stared out. For months, years even, he'd gazed out this window, longing for the day he could buy the Pierson land. That day was on the horizon. Since the recent sale of this year's calf crop, the down payment was in the bank.

"You're going to give her your savings, aren't you?"

Nate hitched both shoulders. "I don't want to argue about it, Pop."

Saving that amount again would take years. Years of calf crops and careful living.

He heard the shuffle of chair against tile and then the movement as his grandfather came up behind him. A strong hand clapped him on the shoulder. "I figure Miss Rainy will give you a fit or two, but you'll get no argument from me. I'm proud of you, son."

Yeah, well, Nate wasn't proud. He was shaken to the core. Sometimes he wondered if he was losing his mind.

"I'm not planning to tell her. She knows how much I want that land. She'd never agree. If the lawyer is paid by an anonymous member of the church, there won't be a thing she can do about it. Helping Rainy is the only thing that feels right. I know the idea sounds crazy, but I have to give her this. I need to."

"Prayed about it, I guess."

Nate made a noise in his throat. "All night. For days. The court date is next week. She has to retain a lawyer soon or give up her dream of adopting Katie."

"You're giving up a dream, too."

He knew that, and he knew it would hurt. But he would hurt a lot more if he didn't do this for Rainy. "There's lots of land. There's only one Katie."

"And only one Rainy."

"Yes, sir. Only one."

"I think that's called love, son." Pop squeezed his shoulder. "Bank closes at three."

The custody hearing wasn't what she'd expected.

There was no jury, only a judge and a couple of court

workers, along with the attorneys, social services personnel and the parties involved. Unlike television trials, there were no histrionics, no great dramatic pauses, only a businesslike discussion of the facts surrounding Katie's life and that of her birth mother.

Rainy tried to listen to the proceedings, but she was so nervous her head roared and words turned to fog before she could absorb them.

Every few minutes, Nate squeezed her hand. She was thankful for his stalwart presence, just as she was thankful for the unexpected gift someone from the church had given by paying all of her attorney fees and court costs. An anonymous donor, her lawyer had said. She'd prayed a thousand blessings upon that generous, godly person.

The overzealous air conditioning unit made her shiver. Or maybe she shivered because of the nerves.

Legal voices droned on, asking questions, presenting documents and affidavits. Paper rustled and a woman coughed.

Rainy glanced across the narrow aisle at the cougher, Michelle Wagner, Katie's birth mother. Thin and very pale, the young woman resembled Katie, with blue eyes and a tilted nose, though her hair was a dull dishwater blond instead of a vibrant red. None of that mattered much. What mattered was Katie. The child had no understanding of what was transpiring here today. From the half dozen screaming sessions today, Katie suspected something was up, but she didn't know her future hung in the balance inside this room filled with strangers. Thank goodness, a social worker sat outside the courtroom with her, shielding her from the testimonies.

Witnesses on behalf of Katie's birth mother, including a psychologist, testified that she was emotionally healthy and stable, completely rehabilitated from her drug habit, and well able to care of Katie. She had an apartment, a job, and a therapeutic accountability group. If the witnesses were correct,

Michelle was getting her life together. Part of Rainy was happy for the woman. Part of her was scared out of her mind.

Mary Chadwick, Rainy's social worker, took the stand and spoke in glowing terms about Rainy as a foster parent. Rainy smiled her thanks.

Then the Wagner attorney began to ask questions. Rainy's spirits tumbled as the lawyer extracted testimony about the complaints filed with DHS about Rainy, complaints from Kathy Underkircher. The social worker, looking distressed, glanced first to Rainy's lawyer, then to Rainy, and back to the judge. In clear tones, she tried to explain away the constant telephone complaints and the police visits to Rainy's home, but the damage was done.

Nausea rolled in Rainy's stomach. She was going to lose Katie. All because of Kathy's animosity. She must have made a sound because Nate shifted toward her with a questioning look. She shook her head and gazed down at her hands, which she was twisting in her lap.

Other testimonies came and went until Rainy's head throbbed and she wondered if the tension in her chest would explode.

At last the verdict was rendered.

While the court recognized and applauded the commitment and care given by foster mother, Rainy Jernagen, the birth mother, Michelle Wagner, had proven herself to the courts. It was the court's opinion that in the interest of the child, Katie Wagner was best served by living with her biological parent. Therefore, she was to be remanded to the custody of her mother, Michelle Wagner, effective immediately.

The single slam of the judge's gavel was like a fist in Nate's gut. Beside him Rainy slumped, too stunned at first to react. Then she began to shake.

Nate slid an arm around her shoulders. She didn't look

up. She sat hunched over, head down, trembling enough to break his heart.

Across the aisle, a shriek of victory rose from Michelle Wagner. She flung herself into the open arms of a woman identified during the hearing as her sister.

What was the matter with that judge? Couldn't he see that Rainy was a better parent to Katie than this other woman could ever be?

But the decision was made. Rainy's lawyer was gathering papers, layering them into his briefcase. Feet shuffled, people exited the courtroom, voices rose and fell.

With a bracing inhale, a stricken Rainy ran her hands down her skirt and stood. Her eyes glowed with pain, but she didn't cry. The attorney and Mrs. Chadwick hurried toward her.

"I'm so sorry, Rainy," the social worker said, her face wreathed in dismay.

"Thank you for trying. You did the best you could. I don't blame you." She swallowed, her lips trembling. "You will keep a close eye on Katie, won't you?"

"Of course I will. Social Services is very diligent in such cases."

Rainy nodded numbly as the woman moved away to talk with the opposing group.

Rainy shook hands with her attorney, who also apologized. From her expression, she didn't want to hear it. She mumbled, "Thank you."

Nate wanted to say a lot more to the man, but he kept his peace. It wasn't the attorney's fault the courts had sided with the birth mother. Right or wrong, this was the norm.

Instead, Nate kept a light hand at Rainy's back, letting her know he was there if she needed him. She hadn't asked him to come today. She hadn't asked anyone to be with her, but Nate had come just the same. She needed him.

"I have to talk to her," she said to no one in particular.

Though visibly shaking, her face pale, she straightened her shoulders and moved toward Michelle Wagner. The other woman momentarily shrank back, wary. Mrs. Chadwick, who now stood conversing with the Wagners, put a hand on Rainy's arm as if to stop her from approaching Katie's mother. Rainy shook her off with a nod of reassurance.

"It's okay, Mrs. Chadwick. I mean no harm, but I need to speak with Ms. Wagner for a minute."

Nate watched in awe as a hurting but composed Rainy quietly introduced herself and said, "Katie is a very special little girl. She has been a gift in my life. I will never forget her."

There was no hostility, only tenderness and compassion, in Rainy's soft-spoken words.

Michelle Wagner slid a nervous gaze to her lawyer and back to Rainy. She swallowed but said nothing.

"I wish you every happiness," Rainy went on, and Nate was sure he'd never witnessed such decency and courage. "Truly. I'll be praying every day for you to be the mother Katie needs."

The other woman found her voice then. "I want to be."

"I know you do." Tears gathered, but didn't fall, as Rainy reached inside her handbag and withdrew a small hand puppet. "Whenever she gets upset and screams, this seems to comfort her. I put it on my hand and make funny pig noises while Piggy kisses her hair and cheeks and…" Her voice wobbled to silence.

"Thank you," Michelle whispered. "Thank you for all you've done to help Katie."

When Rainy's voice shook, Nate slipped her hand into his. "It was my complete and great pleasure. I love her."

With unshed tears glimmering, she gave a brief nod and, with heartbreaking dignity, exited the courtroom.

Chapter Twelve

She could still hear Katie screaming.

On the lonely drive home from the courthouse, Rainy played the scene over and over in her head. For Katie's sake, to ease the transition, the powers that be had allowed Rainy to talk to the child outside the courtroom. Everything had gone fine until Katie's mother took her by the hand and led her toward the exit, leaving Rainy behind. When Katie realized what was happening, she had screamed...and screamed...and screamed.

Rainy had nearly collapsed.

Without Nate's strong shoulder to lean on, she wasn't sure how she would have managed. Without platitudes or empty words, he'd offered to drive her home, to get her something to drink, to do anything she needed. Upon her refusal, he'd walked her to the minivan and watched as she pulled away.

She prayed all the way home, asking the Lord to comfort and protect Katie. She'd also prayed for herself, to make some sense of all that had happened.

Now, she felt as if she'd swallowed a hot air balloon. Her chest was tight, her throat burned with unshed tears, and she wanted to disappear into the great somewhere and never return.

She couldn't, of course. For the sake of the other children she had to keep her composure. They'd be upset, frightened even. They'd need her reassurance. She felt helpless, knowing her reassurance could only go so far. No one could promise them the one thing they'd want to hear.

She pulled into her driveway and shut off the motor. As she stepped out of the van, her mother drove in behind her. With a sob of relief, Rainy gave in to the tears she'd been holding back since the verdict came down.

In another minute, her mother's arms were around her, and they were walking into the house.

"I'm sorry, sweetheart. I know your heart was set on adopting Katie."

Rainy wilted onto the couch, her forehead in her hands, staring down at the carpet. Her eyes clouded again at the sight of a pale pink Kool-Aid stain. Katie had spilled the drink there two nights ago. Afterward, she'd knelt right here on this spot with Rainy and scrubbed and scrubbed with a sponge, trying to clear away the stain. "I'm going to miss her so much."

"Daddy and I wanted her, too, you know. For a grand-daughter. Now we have to trust that the Lord has something else in mind for her."

"I know. Since this began, I've prayed that the outcome would be whatever is best for Katie. I have to accept that this is the right thing. I don't like the decision, but I have to accept it."

"Why didn't you call me last night?" her mother said in mild admonishment. "I would have gone to court with you."

"I didn't want to worry you. I was hoping…" She let the rest go. They both knew what she'd been hoping for. "How did you find out? How did you know?"

"Nate called me. Told me what was going on. He thought you needed your mother. I'd say he was right." In her ener-getic manner, Mom bustled into the kitchen, returning with a glass of last night's leftover iced tea. "Here, drink this. Tea makes everything more palatable."

Bemused, Rainy took the glass but only stared into the cloudy mixture. "Nate called you? When?"

Mom checked her watch, a diamond bracelet affair Dad had given her on their twenty-fifth wedding anniversary. "More than an hour ago, I'd say. Such a nice young man. Very concerned about you."

Nate had excused himself at one point after the verdict came in. She hadn't realized he was sneaking off to call her mother. The thoughtfulness of his gesture eased some of her sadness.

No wonder she was in love with him.

The knowledge had come softly, slowly, but today in the courtroom with him beside her, stalwart and strong, the real meaning of love had settled over her like a warm flannel blanket, secure and comforting.

"I love him, Mom," she said, as if the beautiful words could erase some of the day's sorrow.

"Rainy Nicole!" Her mother's entire countenance brightened. "Oh honey, this is fabulous. Let's go shopping. You need shoes. And you can tell me all about this fabulous man who has finally won your heart."

Her mother's logic brought a much needed laugh. "Leave it to you to translate falling in love to a reason for shoe shopping."

"Honey, breathing is a reason to shoe shop. You need cheering up. This is a great excuse. Now, go splash some water on your face. I'm buying. A snazzy new pair of heels won't solve the problem, but shopping for them will take your mind off your troubles for a while."

"I can't. The children are at Nate's ranch. I need to go get them."

She didn't want to shop. She wanted to lie on her bed and

stare at the ceiling. She wanted to walk around in the girls' bedroom and touch Katie's belongings. She also faced the painful task of telling the other children about the day's outcome.

"No excuses, darling. You're going. Nate would agree. In fact, he said, and this is a quote, 'Rainy's been strong for everyone else about as long as she should have to. She should take all the time she needs to rest and get herself together.' He'll take care of the kids until you come for them. No rush."

"Nate said all that?"

Lifting her perfectly arched eyebrows, Mom offered a spunky smile. "I think maybe he's in love with you, too."

Rainy's heart fluttered.

"You think?"

Oh, she hoped so. Sometimes, like today, she thought he might be, but at other times he'd back away and she wasn't so sure. She threw her arms around her mother. "Mom, you are the best. Thanks for coming."

And thanks to Nate for intuitively knowing exactly what she needed.

Leaning against a post on his back porch, Nate watched Will, Joshua and Emma as the trio went about their chores and played with their animals. The black and white collie ran circles around them, thrilled as ever with their company. Once in a while, one of the kids would fall to the ground, arms around Yo-Yo's neck for a happy wrestling match and a doggy kiss. The sight squeezed him right in the solar plexus.

The trio looked lopsided without redheaded Katie. The whole world seemed lopsided after today's verdict. He still couldn't believe the judge had ruled against Rainy. Though the birth mother seemed to be getting her act together, anyone with eyes could see Rainy was the best mother for Katie.

Sometimes he wondered if his Christianity went deep

enough, because he'd been tempted to tear into the judge and lawyers the way he would have done ten years ago B.C. That's how he always thought of the time before Christ came into his life. B.C.

He rubbed a hand over his aching chest and blew out a heavy, gusty sigh.

What was going to happen to Rainy when she lost the other three, too? Why did she put herself through this? Why did she take the chance of getting her heart broken over and over again?

He liked these kids. Okay, so he was pretty crazy about them. That was the problem. He couldn't protect them any more than he'd been able to protect Katie. He hated that helpless feeling. He hated the pain on Rainy's face and the empty place in his own heart. He hated that moment when Katie was taken away screaming and he hadn't been able to do a thing to save her.

Using the toe of his boot, he kicked at a flat rock. Helpless. Angry. Sad.

There was nothing he could do. Nothing. Even if he'd punched everyone in the courtroom, he couldn't have changed a thing.

No wonder he wrestled so much with the Lord's will for his life. Sometimes the old Nate tried to take over. Sometimes the new Nate thought God was too hard.

He was gonna miss that little redhead. Miss her funny face and her freckles. Miss her giggle.

Kicking out again, he missed the rock and connected only with air. Story of his life. Kicking at air, coming away empty.

With ranch work, the impending loss of the Pierson lease, and his brother and sister, he had enough to worry about without adding kids to the mix. He'd never, ever wanted to go there. Then Rainy had come charging into his life, all velvet and steel and sweetness, and he'd wanted to be her everything. Lately, he'd even begun to think he might enjoy being a dad.

There it was, plain and simple. He wanted to be something he could never be. As a result, he'd failed—again.

After today, when Katie had screamed her way out of the courthouse and Rainy had crumpled in his arms, Nate had faced the truth. He could never be enough for anyone. Hadn't he learned that lesson with Janine and Blake…and Christine? No matter what he did, it was never enough to make things right.

He'd foolishly thought he could make a difference in his siblings' lives. He'd thought the same thing with Rainy and her adorable passel of foster kids.

He'd thought wrong.

The door behind him opened and he heard the approach of footsteps. Nate recognized the slow, heavy boot shuffle as his work-weary granddad. Pop had spent the afternoon repairing a fence break in a water gap along the east side of ranch.

"You're looking mighty grim." Pop scraped a metal lawn chair away from the house with one hand and cradled a cup of coffee with the other. "I reckon things didn't go the way you'd hoped."

"The court ruled for the birth mother."

Pop hissed through his teeth. "Bad deal. Rainy's heart-broken."

It was a statement, not a question. "Devastated."

"You, too."

He didn't want to be, but his granddad knew him too well, sometimes better than he knew himself. "The whole thing stinks. The system stinks. Why take a budding rose from a greenhouse and put her in a dark cellar?"

"The Word says God has a plan for each of us, Nate boy. We have to trust that our prayers will cover Katie."

Trust. Nate was having a hard time with that today. He was

a man of action. Taking care of people was his job. When he couldn't do that job, his imagination went crazy with worry about all the bad things that could happen.

Because, as he well knew, bad things *did* happen to good people.

"Why aren't you with Rainy?" Pop blew across the top of his coffee cup. Steam curled up from the potent black brew.

He'd tried to be. She'd turned him away. "She preferred to be alone. Said she needed time to process."

"You should've stayed with her anyway." Pop took a sip of his coffee and then propped his boot heel on the bottom rung of the porch rail and studied the scuffed, pointed toes. "Women are like that sometimes. They say one thing but mean another. Woman like Rainy wouldn't want to put you out."

Nate hadn't considered that angle. "I phoned her mother."

"A woman needs her man in times like this."

Nate slowly turned his head. "Don't do that, Pop."

His granddad held his gaze steady for several long, telling seconds. Nate's insides twisted and turned, flapping around like a kite in a hurricane. Sometimes he struggled between doing what was right and what he wanted. Sometimes he didn't know the difference. God had sent these kids into his life for a reason. He'd thought that reason was more penance for his mistakes. But he hadn't bargained on taking them and their foster mother into his heart and then letting them all down. Because, like it or not, that's what he'd end up doing.

"Do the young ones know yet?" Pop asked, hitching his chin toward the trio playing freeze tag with each other and Yo-Yo. The dog, of course, did not cooperate in the least and cocked his head in bewilderment at the sudden frozen status of his playmates. The baby goat had joined the fray, dashing this way and that, *bah-ing* with happy abandon. Today, Emma had tied a red bow around his neck and painted his toenails the same color. The ridiculous look would have cheered him any other time.

"They're bound to suspect something, but Rainy wants to tell them later, when she has her own emotions under control. She's making appointments with their counselors tomorrow."

"Smart gal, that Rainy."

Nate shifted his long body, feeling the hard, rough cedar porch timbers poke through the material of his shirtsleeve. "I have to let them go, Pop. To end it."

His grandfather knew him well enough to understand. He dropped his booted foot to the concrete porch and leaned forward, his coffee cup balanced on one knee. "Don't let something like this ruin what you and Rainy have going."

"It's for the best." Pop knew his sins. No reminders required.

"You regretting the money?"

Nate spun around, glaring. "No way. The lawyer was up front with me about our chances of winning. I knew the risk."

"Maybe that's what's eating you. You lost the case, lost Katie, lost the money, lost the land next door."

Nate hadn't looked at the situation that way. "I don't want to see Rainy hurt anymore."

"Then don't hurt her."

"This same scenario could happen again. Those three out there could be taken away from her. No matter how hard you hang on to someone, no matter how hard you try to take care of them, they can be taken away, and there is not a thing you can do to stop the heartache."

"Don't confuse what happened to Christine with these children, Nate boy."

Nate squeezed his eyes shut against the sharp twist of agony. Across the yard, Yo-Yo yipped a happy bark, and blond Emma giggled. Christine had been a little girl like that once, giggly and energetic and full of big-eyed charm. He'd been her big brother, her protector. Yet when she'd needed him most, he'd let her down.

Now he felt as though he'd let Rainy and Katie down, too, though there was nothing he could have done to change the verdict.

To his way of thinking, he wasn't good for Rainy and the children, and he never would be.

"I'm not what they need."

"What exactly is it that they need?"

"Someone who can take care of them. Love them. Be there for them." Someone like Guy Bartlett.

"From my point of view, you've been doing a pretty good job of it. Look out there, Nate boy." Pop waved a hand at the children. "Look at those young 'uns. Happy and free as robins in spring."

But one little redbird was missing. Though he knew he wasn't responsible for that turn of events, Nate felt guilty anyway.

He'd failed in taking care of Christine, and from the looks of things, he was failing miserably in taking care of his surviving siblings. No matter what he did to help them, they always needed more than he could give.

Rainy and her charges would be better off without him, without the baggage he carried, without the never-ending stress that Janine and Blake and his own mind pressed upon him and everyone he touched.

Heart heavy, he shoved his hands in his pockets and struggled to find a way to let go of Rainy Jernigan. It would be the hardest thing he'd ever done, but for his sanity and her well-being, he had to find a way.

Chapter Thirteen

A week passed and for Rainy, the house was brutally empty without Katie's freckled face and squeaky voice. The other children solemnly accepted the change, saying little. According to the counselor, they'd suffered so many losses, they'd come to expect the worst.

Their greatest concern was that they, too, would have to leave Rainy's care. Unfortunately, no one could promise them permanence, but Rainy had her lawyer on the job, doing everything possible to expedite the adoption. She'd been able to give them that much.

Yet, they clung more, wanted her closer. Joshua had bad dreams and Will became overvigilant, as if he knew Rainy couldn't safeguard his siblings anymore and the job had become his again.

She ached for him and prayed more than she'd ever prayed before, for the kids, for herself, for Nate, too.

Something had happened to him after the hearing. For a couple of days, he'd been so attentive in his efforts to cheer her. She knew he'd been devastated at Katie's loss, though he'd never said as much. He'd been quieter, lost in thought, the way she often was.

Now, she was noticing a new difference in him that hadn't been there before. A distancing, as if he was trying to pull away from their relationship. They'd never spoken about the subtle change. Rainy was almost afraid to ask. She'd been so happy about falling in love, so committed to growing their relationship. She wondered if she'd done something wrong.

For the past two days, he'd been absent when she'd driven to the ranch to pick up the children. According to Pop, he was helping Janine move to a new apartment. Understandable. Janine constantly needed something or the other from her brother.

Yet when Rainy had telephoned him last night, he'd been unusually quiet and the conversation had dwindled away to nothing in a matter of minutes. Gone were the hour-long talks about anything and everything.

Perhaps he was worried about his sister. Or maybe he, too, still struggled to process the pain of losing Katie. Didn't men handle emotion differently than women?

A take-the-bull-by-the-horns kind of gal, Rainy decided to find out what was going on. Nate had been there when she'd needed him. So, maybe it was his turn to need her.

Rainy planted a new pair of aqua colored high heels in the soft soil outside the tack room. Inside the dimly lit space, Nate sat on an upturned bucket, bridles, halters and other tack strewn around him.

"Pop told me I'd find you here."

The older cowboy had been in the back lot showing the kids how to twirl a lariat. When he'd pointed toward the tack room, he'd had a gleam in his eye Rainy hadn't quite understood.

Nate glanced up, hands paused on a halter rope he was braiding. "Rainy. How you doing?"

Rainy. He'd called her Rainy. He never did that unless the mood was very serious. "The better question is how are you?"

One shoulder twitched. "As you can see, I'm all right."

Shadows troubled his dark eyes and there was something—*something*—he wasn't telling her.

"You don't seem all right." She waited two beats for a reply that never came. "Is it Katie? Are you still upset over what happened?"

He went back to weaving one strip of leather over another. "Aren't you?"

"Of course I am. It will take time to stop missing her." A lot of time, a lot of prayer to soothe the aching hole Katie's departure had created.

"But will you ever stop worrying about her?" Nate's voice deepened with emotion. "Wondering if she's safe? Wondering if her mother is staying on the straight and narrow?"

The questions were a jab at an already vulnerable wound. These were the things she prayed about daily. "I don't know. I keep clinging to the promise that God will never leave nor forsake her. That's all I know to do." She lifted her palms, let them fall. "Sometimes I feel so helpless…."

Nate shot her a look and then went back to the tack repair. So that was the problem. He felt helpless, too. For a strong, independent man such as Nate, feeling helpless was about as bad as it got.

Outside the tack room, one of the horses leaned against the sheet-metal building. The inside wall popped from the pressure. A wood bee buzzed in the sunlit doorway, searching for a place to drill.

Rainy went to her haunches, balancing on her toes in front of Nate. He didn't look up. His fingers continued to braid. Over, under. Over, under.

"Right now, we're all hurting," she said. "But please don't shut me out, Nate. Don't go all silent and brooding on me. We need to talk, to help each other get through this."

"Rainy, I—" He stopped braiding long enough to look at her, his expression pained. "I'm sorry."

Rainy blinked. "Sorry for what? You haven't done anything to be sorry for. What's going on in that head of yours?"

His chest rose and fell in a heavy huff. He put the neatly braided rope aside. "You're right. We do need to talk. Katie isn't the only thing that's bothering me."

Rainy's heart bumped. Something was more wrong than she'd anticipated. "You can talk to me about anything."

One hand rubbed at the front of his shirt. Work-roughened fingers whispered over coarse cotton. He took another deep breath. "I don't know how to say this."

"Straight out works for me."

"I care about you, Rainy—" he started.

She touched his knee. "I care about you too. A lot." Like in l-o-v-e. "You have to know that already."

"I do. That's what bothers me. You shouldn't. I can't."

"You can't what? Come on, Cowboy, you're scaring me. I thought we had something special going. If I'm wrong, say so."

He squeezed his eyes shut for one long moment. Rainy's heart thundered in her ears.

"You're not wrong."

Rainy almost wilted into the dirt with relief. "Then what is the problem?"

"Something we've never discussed and should have. Kids."

"We discuss the kids all the time."

"No. I mean, we've never discussed kids in the future. My fault. I take full responsibility. I should have told you sooner."

Rainy still didn't understand what he was trying to say. "Kids are my life. You know that."

He reached forward, took her upper arms in his strong,

cowboy hands and held her gaze with his. "Kids are *your* life. They aren't mine."

Something shriveled inside. "I don't know what you mean."

"I care about you, Rainy."

"You said that already—"

"Let me finish. I don't want to hurt you or those kids out there. I'm nuts about them. That's the problem."

"You aren't making any sense."

"Then let me be clear." There was something hard in his voice. Rainy's pulse ratcheted upward. Foreboding crept over her like a black fog. Nate's jaw worked, his eyes begged her to understand. But how could she when she didn't know what was wrong?

In a dry whisper, she asked, "What is it, Nate? Please."

"I don't want kids," he said. "Ever."

Nate watched Rainy's confusion turn to shock. Slowly, she shook her head from side to side, as if denying the truth she hadn't wanted to hear. Nate thought he might die of self-reproach. He deserved to die. He never should have let things go this far. He should have been honest from the start. He'd foolishly believed he could be with her and never have to pay the consequences.

"You're not making sense." Her bottom lip quivered. "Everyone wants kids."

"I've had kids all my life, Rainy. I would have told you from the beginning, but I never expected to—"

Hurt radiated off her like sun off a metal roof. "To what?"

Love you. Love you so much that I can't take the risk of ruining your life.

But he couldn't say that now, so instead, he said, "Get…attached to all of you."

Nate wasn't sure what reaction he expected, but it wasn't

the one he got. She shoved his arms away and pushed up, stalked to the open door, looked out and then spun around.

"Nate Del Rio, that is the weakest excuse, as well as the most idiotic statement, I have ever heard. If you are tired of me and want me to go away, be man enough to tell me. But don't concoct some ridiculous tale."

Oh, man. Tired of her? He couldn't get enough of her. The day went on forever until the moment she sailed in, lighting up the place with her bright smile and brighter ideas.

Floundering, he said, "That's not it at all. Rainy, listen—"

But she was past listening. She stabbed a finger in the air. "Nothing you've said makes the least bit of sense. You say you love the kids, but you are *too* attached to them. What does that mean? Then in the next sentence you say you never want kids. How can you love kids and not want them? Tell me that."

"You don't understand."

"You got that right, Cowboy." When her eyes grew suspiciously bright and she tottered on the ridiculously high pair of blue heels, Nate nearly crumpled. He wanted to pull her close, to tell her that he didn't mean it. But he resisted the urge. Honesty in a relationship was essential.

Even if they didn't have a relationship. Which they didn't. They couldn't.

Yes, he was one confused dude.

"Will you listen to what I have to say?" he asked, almost desperately now that he'd made a mess of things. He took her hand, tugged. Her soft skin, normally warm, felt ice cold.

"You know I will," she said and touched his cheek.

Of course she would. Rainy always listened. It was one of her gifts, one of the things he loved about her.

"I need to tell you something. Something that I hope will make you understand why I feel the way I do about being a father." he said. "Come in the barn, where we can sit and talk in private."

He didn't want an audience during this conversation, and the kids and Pop would come looking for them soon.

Still holding her hand, and surprised that she'd let him, he led the way through the outdoor lot and into the huge area inside the hay barn where large square bales of prairie grass piled to the ceiling.

Some kind of bird—a swallow, he thought—was nesting in the rafters. The creature flapped wildly, swooped a dive-bombed warning over their heads, then disappeared into the blue sky.

Rainy perched on a hay bale, shoulders tense. Hope and confusion radiated from her in equal amounts. Nate felt like the jerk he was. The best he could hope for was her under-standing. If she hated him, he deserved it. He swallowed, his throat as dry as trail dust.

He'd kept Christine's death bottled up for so long, he couldn't find the words.

"You look as if you're going before the firing squad," Rainy said softly. "It can't be that bad, can it?"

He sucked in a lungful of grass-scented air, exhaling in a gust. "Yes, it can. It is. I've never talked to anyone about this before. Except Pop."

And they didn't really talk about that awful time. They tiptoed around it.

Her fingers pressed into his forearm. "You don't have to tell me."

Her kindness was killing him.

"Yes, I do. I want you to understand why I can't have kids. That it's not you. It's not the kids. It's me. It's what I did and what I have to do." He picked at a piece of hay, pulled it loose from the bale. "You've met my sister Janine, and you know about Blake, my brother."

Her chin dipped in agreement. "You have a nice family."

He made a noise in the back of his throat. "They're pains in the neck."

Amusement eased her worried features. "But you love them."

"Yeah, I do. I loved Christine, too." The name slid off his tongue easily, but the taste was bittersweet.

Rainy cocked her head, amusement fleeing as she intuitively went on alert. "Who's Christine?"

"Christine—" his throat worked "—was my baby sister."

Rainy's eyes registered the verb tense. Her fingers tightened on his arm, a subtle touch of encouragement. "Was?"

He nodded. Was. Past tense. Gone forever.

"What happened?"

His gut clenched. "She was murdered."

The ugly words hung in the warm barn, as grievous now as then.

"Oh, no. *Nate*." The horror in Rainy's voice matched the guilt in his heart, but Rainy-like, she scooted close, looped her hands around his elbow and leaned her forehead against his shoulder in a brief hug.

Just that little bit of tenderness melted him. How did a man get the courage to break away from such a woman?

"What happened? Who would do such a terrible thing?"

Holding back a tidal wave of emotion, he told her the basics, the words shooting out in staccato rhythm.

"She was hitchhiking. A monster offered her a ride. Three days later a hunter found her body. In a shallow grave. In the woods." His fingers bit into the rough fabric of his jeans. "She was nineteen. And beautiful." He shook his head, remembering. "Nineteen."

"Dear Jesus," Rainy murmured, and he knew the words were a prayer. For him. She gazed a spot somewhere behind him deep in thought. "I can't imagine what your family has suffered."

Suffered. Yes, they'd suffered.

"Because of me. She died, and they all suffered—because of me."

Rainy's gaze snapped back to his. "That is not true."

"I wish it wasn't, but it is. She had car trouble." He scrubbed his hands over his face. "She was always having some kind of crisis."

"The way Janine and Blake do now?"

He nodded. "She called me from the side of the highway, wanted me to come pick her up and fix her car. I'd warned her before she left that her car needed repair and shouldn't be driven. She hadn't listened. She never listened to me. Until that phone call."

"What do you mean?"

"I mean," he said, his voice raspy with contained emotion, "I told her that I was tired of running to her aid. The stalled car was her problem. Not mine. I didn't care if she had to hitchhike to the nearest garage." He tilted his head and looked up into the rafters. "I told her that, Rainy. I said the words that sent her straight into the hands of a murderer."

"You had no way of knowing what would happen. You can't blame yourself."

"No? Well, I do. It's my fault she's dead. If I had done my job… If I had answered her cry for help…" He squeezed his eyes shut at the brutal onslaught of crime photos flickering through his head. "She died because her brother was too busy watching a football game."

More than anything, Rainy wanted to comfort this broken man. Once again, she slid her arms around his shoulders, resting her cheek against his shirtfront. Nate's heart thundered beneath her ear. His chest rose and fell like a man in torment.

She couldn't begin to imagine what the Del Rios had experienced. Nothing that heinous had ever happened in her own family. Thank God. But now, some of Nate's behaviors became crystal clear. No wonder he worried about the children getting hurt on the ranch. No wonder he pampered his sister and brother as if they were helpless ten-year-olds.

"The man who took her life is solely to blame. No one else." Soothingly, she stroked her fingers over his whisker-rough cheek. "You are not responsible."

He turned his head so that they faced one another, whisper close, his tormented soul visible in his eyes.

"I wish I believed that, but I don't. If I had answered her call, she would be alive today."

"And you're still punishing yourself, letting the guilt eat you up."

"I let her die, Rainy. My baby sister. A person's life is a lot to make up for."

"Is that what you're doing? Trying to make up for her death? Is that why you jump every time Blake or Janine call?"

"Can you blame me? What if I don't respond and history repeats itself?"

"They're adults now, not teenagers. They can take care of themselves."

"You don't think families should help one another?"

"Of course I do. That's not what I meant, and you know it. They take advantage of you, Nate. Even Pop thinks so."

He pulled away from her and bolted upright. The muscle beneath his eye jerked as he stared blindly at the dust motes dancing around his scuffed boots. From her spot on the hay bale, Rainy battled with the need to comfort him and the conflicting need to shake him out of the past.

After a long, troubled moment, she said, "I'm confused. I don't understand what all this has to do with kids. With why you don't ever want to have children."

His shoulders raised and lowered, but he didn't turn back to her. "I can't be what you need, Rainy. Don't you get it? I couldn't take care of Christine. I'm doing a lousy job with Janine and Blake." He was doing a lousy job with Crossroads Ranch, as well, but he didn't want her to know about that. "I'd be a lousy father, too."

He heard the rustle of movement behind as she came to stand beside him, twining her arm through his. She felt good there, as though she belonged by his side.

"You know what?" she said, tugging gently on his elbow, her voice soft and sympathetic. "Losing Katie was hard. But I'm going to survive. I'm going to go on loving and giving and doing what I can to make a difference. I can't just curl up and quit."

"I don't see your point."

"The point is, what happened to your sister is too terrible for words. But, Nate, it happened, and you can't change it. You have to do what I have to do with Katie. Give the pain to God and let it go. Move on with your life, be the best you can be in her memory, but let her go. You didn't die with your sister."

Nate jerked away, stunned that a woman as kind and understanding as Rainy would say such a cruel thing.

"You have no idea what you're talking about," he said, his jaw tight enough to break a molar. "I'm to blame for my sister's death. That's a far cry from a custody dispute."

"You're being ridiculous." Her voice rose, her eyes snapping. "You did not kill her any more than you make bad choices for Janine and Blake. They make them for themselves. You aren't accountable for them."

"You're wrong."

"And you're sounding like Will. Stop being a martyr, Nate. Stop thinking the world depends on you to take care of it. That's God's job. You have so much to offer, so much to give, but not like this. Get over the past and move on."

Now she'd gone too far. No caring human being ever got over the murder of a loved one. Ever. Drawing on hurt and anger, he said the words that would set her free.

"The kids still have projects. I won't deny them that. I won't be here, Rainy. I'm done. We're done."

And before he could fall on his knees and beg her forgiveness, he stalked away.

Chapter Fourteen

Devastated, her heart bleeding all over the place, Rainy somehow managed to gather the children together to leave. Nate had disappeared into the house, and she wasn't about to follow him inside for a repeat performance. His parting message had been as clear and cold as glacial water. They were done. The beautiful emotion growing between them would never blossom into full flower. He wanted nothing to do with her anymore.

Maybe the relationship had been her imagination all along. Maybe he'd never cared one whit for her or the children.

But he did. She knew he did. He'd even admitted as much.

Right before he'd tossed her out.

Blindly shoving the car key into the slot, her hands shook.

Rainy didn't want to cry in front of the children, but they all knew something was wrong from the moment they'd climbed into the van to drive home.

"Are you mad at us, Miss Rainy?" Joshua inquired, his blue eyes too big for his face.

With one hand gripping the steering wheel, she patted him reassuringly with the other. "No, darling. You're the best kids in the universe."

She was positive Nate thought the kids were fabulous, too.

Perhaps she should have kept her mouth shut. Maybe she'd gone too far. Who was she to tell him how to fix his life?

The woman who loved him, that was who. As such, she felt a responsibility to tell him the truth. Hanging on to his guilt had done nothing but hurt him and make parasites out of Janine and Blake.

A part of her wanted to turn the van around, go back to the Crossroads, and tell him she'd been wrong. But she wasn't. She was sorry for upsetting him, even more sorry for what his family had endured, but she wasn't wrong. He needed to let his past go and embrace the future. The decision, though, was his. All she could do now was pray for him.

And for her own aching heart.

Nate couldn't sleep. Long after midnight, he dressed and let himself quietly out the back door. Yo-Yo, curled into a comma on the porch, awoke and raised his head in question.

"Go back to sleep, buddy," Nate said softly.

But of course, the dog rose, shook himself, stretched and sidled up to nudge his head beneath Nate's hand. By habit, Nate rubbed the warm, soft neck, taking mild comfort from a pal who demanded nothing but love.

Rainy wanted too much.

And he simply did not have it in him.

The night was cool and soft, scented with dogwood blooms, and lit by an impossible number of glimmering stars against a black chalkboard sky.

God was up there, he thought, as he stood with his head tilted back. Tonight, he needed to be close to God, to know the Lord was his Father, not just his Master and King.

Without much consideration, he ambled to the barn and

saddled Moccasin, the sure-footed old Palomino who could find his way blindfolded around the Crossroads. With Yo-Yo trotting happily alongside, he rode out into the pasture, passed the gates, passed the black, lumpy shadows that were cattle and onto the Pierson lease.

In a matter of months he'd have to find a new lease or sell some of his stock. He wanted to resent the loss, but he couldn't. When he'd told Pop he believed Rainy and Katie were worth the money, he'd meant it. They were worth everything. Couldn't Rainy understand? She was valuable, special. He could never be the man she deserved. If money could bring Katie back into her life, he would gladly sell everything he owned to make it happen.

Their conversation from this afternoon swirled around inside him, painful and cutting. He'd thought she would understand. Janine and Blake needed his influence as well as his help. He couldn't turn his back on them.

He rode on, slowly dawdling along the creek bank where recent spring rains caused the water to flow musically, trickling over rocks and roots. A hoot owl called. To the Native Americans in the area, the owl's cry was bad luck. Nate didn't believe that, but the lonely sound added to his melancholia.

After a while, he prayed, spilling out his confusion and anguish. Rainy had no right to say the things she'd said. She had no way of knowing what his life was like or how he felt to know his indifference had caused Christine's death.

After a while, he sagged in the saddle, physically weary but still mentally tangled. The Lord didn't have any answers for him tonight.

He rode back to the barn to put the horse away, giving him a handful of sweet feed for his efforts. Hands in his pockets, Nate strode toward the house. Yo-Yo dogged his heels, a silent, unobtrusive, accepting companion.

The back porch light flared on. He blinked, blinded for a second.

"Something wrong, Nate boy?" Pop stood in the open back door.

No use avoiding the inevitable. His granddad knew him too well. Anytime Nate took a night ride, something was troubling him.

"Didn't mean to wake you," he said, stepping up into the light. A frog hopped across his boot and out into the darkness. Yo-yo gave the critter a glance but didn't bother. Instead, the collie flopped, with a sigh, into his corner of the porch and curled up with his head on his paws, facing the men.

Pop arched his shoulders in an awakening stretch and scratched at the back of his head. "You want some coffee?"

"Are you serious? I can't sleep, Pop. Coffee will only make matters worse."

"If you can't sleep anyway, you might as well have a hot jolt of java." He motioned toward the inside. "I got a fresh pot perking."

"Motor oil," Nate mumbled as he slid into one of the metal lawn chairs.

"I heard that."

They both chuckled softly.

"So, are you going to tell me what happened between you and Rainy?"

Nate cocked an eyebrow. "Think you're smart, don't you?"

"I seen her tear out of here this evening without the usual lollygagging the two of you do."

"We don't lollygag."

Pop made a rude noise. "Lying's a sin."

"Leave me alone, Pop."

"Not until you tell me what's going on. I kind of had my heart set on that girl."

So had he. "It's not going to work out."

The admission was harder to make than he'd expected. A lot harder. In the next few minutes, accompanied by the sound of Yo-Yo's snore and the occasional low of contented cattle, Nate told his granddad about the conversation.

Pop listened without interruption. When he finished, the older man pushed off the porch post and shuffled inside the house, returning with two oversized mugs of black, black coffee.

"Drink this," he said, handing a mug to Nate. "It'll put hair on your chest."

Nate's mouth twitched. Pop had told him that same thing years ago when he was a teenager, longing to grow up.

Hands wrapped around the warm cup, he took a sip, then grimaced. "Pond sludge."

Pop grinned, delighted. "Good stuff. Rivals those fancy espresso places."

"Right. Pond sludge latte. Gotta be a top seller."

They sipped in companionable silence, Nate glad to have his granddad's company. Brooding alone hadn't helped.

After a bit, Pop loudly slurped at his coffee, a signal that he was about to speak.

"Rainy's right, Nate boy."

Nate bristled but didn't reply.

"When Christine died—"

"She was murdered, Pop." Nate's hand flexed on the mug handle. "She didn't just die."

Pop waved off the comment. Once the old man started, he was going to have his say. Might as well let him.

"No one needs to tell me, son. I know what happened. That's not the point. The point is this. When she died, you got some wild-haired notion that you could have saved her."

"I could have."

"Nope. You couldn't. Get that settled in your hard Del Rio

head. I don't know why we had to lose Christine, but we did. You didn't cause her murder, but you've spent years paying for it as if you had. I see what you do. I know why you do it. All of it."

Nate had no idea what Pop was talking about, but he was getting more uncomfortable by the second. He took another sip of fortifying pond sludge.

"Here's what I think, Nate boy." Pop drained his cup with an *ahhh* and plunked the stoneware onto the concrete porch. "You got a works mentality."

Nate tilted his head, figuring Pop would explain himself. He did.

"That means you think you got to work your way into God's good graces, especially when it comes to Janine and Blake. But the same goes for Rainy's kids and the Handyman Ministry, and a host of other things you do."

"The Bible teaches us to serve others."

"Not as a way of winning God's favor. Scripture says we're saved by grace, not by works. The Lord loves you because you're His, not because you sacrifice your own happiness for your brother and sister."

"I like helping people." Most of the time.

"Nothing wrong with that. It's the motive that counts. In here." Pop tapped a thick finger to his breast bone. "We both know you resent the way Janine and Blake expect you to drop everything and come running."

That much was true. He loved them and worried about them, but he resented their dependence, too. Still, they were his brother and sister. He was the oldest. If he didn't look after them, who would?

"God doesn't blame you for Christine's death, son. Neither does anyone else. Don't you think it's time to stop blaming yourself, let go of the past and take hold of the good things God's trying to give you?"

Nate's gut knotted. He wanted to believe Pop was right. With all his heart, he wanted to believe. But he didn't.

Rainy cranked the volume on the CD player as she made the turn onto the graveled road leading to Crossroads Ranch. Her favorite Christian group, Third Day, belted out, "Don't you know I've always loved you," an encouraging reminder that God's love and grace were sufficient. No matter how sad she was about the loss of both Nate and Katie, God was still right here, surrounding her with his eternal, overwhelming love.

Determined to be happy, to embrace the good, she smiled through tears at the heavens. Though some might think her silly, she waved at the sky and said, "Thank you, Father."

Peace in the storm was not just a phrase preachers tossed around, but a reality to Rainy. She'd never understood before, but now she did. Oddly enough, the trying days of late had taken her faith to new heights. God was faithful when no one or nothing else was.

As she approached Nate's property line, a sign caught her attention, but she was going too fast to read it. She braked to a stop, dust swirling up around the windshield. Wryly, she thought of the five dollars she'd spent on a car wash yesterday.

She reversed the van, easing backward until she was parallel with the big red and white sign. Country Realty. For Sale.

Third Day kicked into one of her favorites, "Cry Out to Jesus," but she reached over and turned the volume down.

As she stared at the puzzling sign, her eyebrows drew together in a frown. She checked her location again, though she knew very well she was parked in front of the Pierson lease, the property Nate intended to purchase. Why was a For Sale sign needed? Nate had already proclaimed his intention to buy the land. He had the first option. No one else could buy this acreage.

After a few seconds in which she came to no conclusion, she drove on to the ranch to collect the children.

As usual, the black and white collie rushed out to greet her, barking a few times for good measure. To her amusement, Snowflake, who now had the run of the property as if he, too, was a dog, scampered around the side of the long, low house. A small bell jingled from a red collar around his neck.

She parked the van next to the big cedar and got out, knowing that if the animals appeared, the children would not be far behind. Sure enough, all three barreled toward her. Will carried a baseball and bat. Emma wore someone's oversized ball glove on her head. Joshua toted the white ball, skidding to a stop in front of the van to toss it high into the air. Head back, he feinted from side to side, both hands extended until the ball thudded to the ground in front of him.

Will laughed. Rainy hid a grin. "Did the sun get in your eyes?"

"Nope," Joshua said, bending to scoop up the ball. "I just missed it."

Rainy stooped for a hug. "This is your first year to play. You'll get the hang of it."

"He's getting better, Miss Rainy," Emma said. "The ball doesn't hit him on the head anymore."

"Well, there's something to be said for progress." She ruffled Josh's hair and then grabbed each of the other two for their afternoon hug. When she'd first gotten the trio, none of them quite knew what to do with her displays of affection. Now, they expected them and had learned to reciprocate.

"Where's Pop?" she asked.

Just then the older cowboy limped around the house. "I'm coming."

"Why are you limping? Did you hurt your foot again?"

"Ah, it isn't nothing." He waved off the idea of injury. "Twisted my ankle."

"Working with the cattle?" she asked.

"Nope. Chasing a fly ball." He rubbed his chin and chuckled. "That Will's got a power swing on him. Can hit a ball plumb to the pond."

So Pop had been playing ball with the kids. Without thinking better of it, Rainy hugged the older man.

"What was that for?" he asked, looking pleased.

"For being such a nice man."

"Does that mean you'll bring me some of your fancy brownies next time you come?"

The request brought an ache to her heart, but she didn't let it show. The brownies were Nate's favorites. Since the breakup, she'd baked far too many of them. Half the neighborhood, her students and her Sunday School class had benefited from her fits of stress baking. She'd taken them everywhere but here.

"I'd love to make some brownies for you, Pop. You'll have them tomorrow." She motioned toward the van. "Load up, kids. Time to go." Before Nate arrived. Seeing him hurt too much.

"Whoa, now," Pop said. "You can't leave yet. We're in the third inning. Will and Joshua are winning. Me and Emma deserve a chance to catch up."

"What's the score?"

"Twelve to five," Emma said with disgust. "Me and Pop need help."

Rainy pressed her fingertips over her smile. "Oh, my."

"I have an idea, Miss Rainy," Joshua said. "You can play on their team and maybe they'll have a chance. They're good. But Will is like a pro or something."

She noticed the way Will's narrow shoulders straightened at the compliment. This was good for him, building his confidence.

"And I'm a tad bit gimpy," Pop added, his eyes twinkling merrily.

Rainy knew when she was being manipulated, but she didn't mind at all. "How can I refuse? We can't stop a game in the third inning. Lead on, mighty Yankees."

With a whoop of joy, the three kids, followed by a jingling goat and an overzealous collie, started toward the back yard. Rainy and Pop followed at a slower pace.

"Maybe you should go inside and put ice on your ankle," Rainy suggested.

"Nah, it's all right." He waited two beats until the children were out of earshot to say, "So, how you doing, Rainy? I mean, really doing, since all this nonsense with Nate?"

"I'm okay. Sad. Disappointed. But God is closer than ever." She stopped long enough to pull a bright yellow dandelion. "Is Nate okay?"

"Nah, he won't ever be okay until he gets his mind straight. I tried talking to him. He's got a hard head sometimes."

She sighed, rubbed the soft wildflower against her cheek. "Do you think he'll ever realize he wasn't to blame for his sister's death?"

"I'm talking. And praying. Janine and Blake don't help. They keep him burdened down, feeling obligated. He has the fool notion that he's not good enough for you or some such nonsense, that he can't be enough for them and for you and for all these young ones of yours at the same time."

"I know." And she was helpless to change his mind. "He's unhappy. I don't want that for him. I love him, Pop."

He patted her shoulder. "I know you do. I believe he feels the same. That's what's got him in such a turmoil. My grandson's at a Crossroads in more ways that one."

Rainy hoped Pop was right, but she was beginning to have doubts.

They rounded the corner of the house where Will and Joshua were carefully realigning the three bases and home plate. The bases appeared to be pieces of an old horse blanket.

Rainy, still ruminating on Pop's "Crossroads" comment, remembered the troubling For Sale sign.

"I saw something odd on my way out here today," she said.

"Yeah?" Pop removed his hat to swipe a hand over a perspiring and balding head.

"A For Sale sign on the Pierson lease."

Pop plopped the hat in place, his expression changing from interest to wary.

"That place is Nate's dream," Rainy went on. "No one else can buy it out from under him, can they? Why is there a sign up if he has exclusive first option?"

Pop rubbed at his ear, face averted to watch the children. Rainy got a funny, suspicious feeling in her stomach, though she couldn't for the life of her understand why.

"Pop? What's going on with Nate's land?"

The old cowboy shifted his weight onto his good leg. "Well, it's like this, Miss Rainy. Nate let the place go. He's not going to buy it."

"Not buying it? How can that be? He's saved for years to buy that property, to expand, to grow the best organic beef in the state." She thought of the excitement in Nate when he'd told her about the expansion, of the times he'd dreamed out loud, sharing his plans for the future. "This doesn't make sense. Why would he change his mind?"

Again, the silence. When Pop spoke, he seemed to be saying something she couldn't quite comprehend.

"If you really want the answer—and I think you should—you'll have to ask Nate."

Nate wiped a forearm across his sweaty brow. The sun was high and hot this afternoon. He'd spent the day separating cattle and was bone tired. Tired was good. It kept his mind off other troubles. Namely Rainy. He missed her. Missed their talks, their Friday-night movies. Truth was, he missed everything about her.

Will, Joshua and Emma tumbled off the bus each evening full of school news and childhood energy. No matter how hard he tried to let Pop handle them and their projects, the three siblings tracked him down wherever he was.

To make matters worse, Rainy kept right on coming to the Crossroads every night. She and the kids and Pop had a grand time without him. On those chance occasions when their paths crossed, her smile fell away and she gazed at him with hurt in her gray-blue eyes.

He was such a jerk. Surely, she understood that now. Understood that he was not good for her.

But seeing her was a sweet torment that kept him awake at night.

As such, he'd taken to staying away from the ranch or far out in the pasture until dark.

This particular evening, he'd had no choice but to come in from the field. His horse had pulled up lame.

On foot, he led Moccasin through the gates and across the wide, empty lot. From somewhere near the house, he could hear the kids playing, their voices carrying high and joyous on the still air. Yo-Yo yipped happily. The dog was crazy about those kids and had even taken to lying beneath the cross timbers of the ranch each afternoon, waiting for the bus to rumble into view.

A woman laughed, warm and joyful.

Rainy.

The ever-present knot in his belly tightened. He left Moccasin in the stall and walked to the corner of the barn, looking toward the house, where the voices seemed to originate.

He did a double take. There they were, all of them including Pop, playing the craziest game of baseball he'd ever imagined.

The goat, who followed Emma with the same devotion that Yo-Yo gave the boys, dashed down the baseline after the little girl, bleating like crazy. His jingle bell bobbed and tinkled. When it appeared Joshua would catch the ball and put Emma out, Snowflake gave him a hearty butt, knocking him on his backside. Yo-Yo rushed to his defense, alternately barking at Snowflake and licking Joshua's dirty face.

All the players fell down laughing.

Nate laughed, too. He started forward to join the fun, then caught himself and turned back toward the barn and the limping horse.

Some things were better left alone.

Chapter Fifteen

The thunderstorm arose suddenly, as was common in Oklahoma. Though the afternoon had been hot and humid, a harbinger of stormy weather, the dark clouds boiled together in a matter of minutes.

One clap of thunder and a crack of distant lightning sent three wide-eyed children scurrying toward the house from the calf barn. Nate, who'd been stacking sacks of horse feed in the bins watched them run, full-out, legs pumping toward the house. A few seconds later, Pop limped out behind them. The old man refused to see a doctor for his ankle, too, claiming that it, like his foot, would heal in God's time. Before Pop reached the back porch, the dark skies opened with a downpour, soaking him.

The horses stirred in their stalls, restless at the sudden crackle of electrical energy sizzling in the air. A bolt of lightning zigzagged overhead, the accompanying crash of thunder startling and magnificent. Nothing like a good Oklahoma thunderstorm to clear the air. Since boyhood, Nate had enjoyed the wild unpredictability of Oklahoma weather, finding thunderstorms invigorating, exciting.

He finished his task and stood inside the horse barn,

watching water run off the metal roof, breathing in the fresh rain scent, stirred by the awesomeness of nature.

Pop would check the TV for severe weather alerts, but by all signs, this was one of those fast and furious, gone-in-a-few-minutes cloudbursts. The sun would probably be shining before Rainy got here. Even if it wasn't, Rainy brought sunshine with her, from the inside out.

As always, something inside him reacted when he thought about the woman he couldn't have. She'd been wrong to take him to task the way she had, though he was struggling to remain angry. She didn't understand. That was the problem. No one did.

After a few minutes, the rain had not abated and Nate began to worry. Probably better get to the house and make sure there were no tornado warnings. Hand clapped to the top of his hat, he loped the hundred yards to the house. The cold sucked his breath as rain soaked his shirt.

Thunder rumbled. He braced himself for the lightning strike. By the time his boots thumped onto the porch, pea-sized hail pinged against the house and bounced across the yard, dotting the green grass.

The back door opened and Will's face peered out, anxious. "You're gonna get wet."

Nate grinned and shook like a dog. "Already am."

A sprinkled Will jumped back. "Ew."

Amused by the boy's reaction, Nate stepped inside and shucked his boots on the kitchen tile. "Anyone look at the weather on TV?"

"Pop did. He says it's just a thunderstorm. Nothing to worry about."

"Would you grab a towel for me, then?" Nate motioned toward the back of the house, but Will was already gone. He knew where things were. In seconds, the boy returned, tossing the fluffy terry cloth to him.

Patting the excess water from his face and chest, Nate followed Will into the living room. The rest of the crew was scattered about on chairs, on the floor, etc. Emma had curled up with her reading book. Rainy would be glad to see that. Josh stood at the big front windows staring out. Was he worried about the storm? Or watching for Rainy?

"What do you see out there, partner?" Nate asked.

"Hail. Big hail." Joshua tapped a finger on the window-pane "Look at it bouncing around."

"Like golf balls," Will said, going to stand beside his brother.

Nate placed a hand on each child's shoulder. "You boys scared?"

Both shook their heads in denial.

"I think it's kind of cool," Joshua said. "I might want to be a meteor—meterol—a weatherman when I grow up."

"Yeah?" Nate said. "Good plan. I like weather, too."

He'd even considered studying the subject as a profession after high school. That had been before Christine's death, before Janine and Blake had proved themselves inept without him. Not that he regretted his decision to raise cattle instead of going to college. He was happy here. Most of the time.

"Come on, Josh," Will said, tugging on his brother's arm. "Let's go play a game until Rainy comes."

For all his protests to the contrary, Nate figured Will didn't really appreciate the thunder and lightning as much as Joshua did.

"Later," Josh said, fascinated by the show outside his window. "I want to watch the storm."

Will shrugged, looking at Nate as if he thought his little brother was loony, but said, "I'll get a game out. You want Chinese checkers?"

"I don't care." Joshua jerked a shoulder, but didn't take his eyes from the window as he said in awe, "Look at those hail-stones. I wonder how big they are."

Will made another face and headed toward the back of the house, where Nate kept a stack of board games. For some reason, he'd started collecting the things during the past couple of months. He and Rainy had enjoyed a crazy, laugh-filled time playing Scattergories one night.

Annoyed to be thinking of her again, he grumbled. "I gotta change these wet clothes. Pop, will you thaw out something for dinner and put on some fresh coffee?"

Pop shoved off the couch and headed toward the kitchen with a chuckle. "You claim I make terrible coffee."

"You do," Nate called with an answering chuckle just before closing the bedroom door. A rumble of thunder followed him.

As he dressed, the rain abated and a glimmering of light slithered through the mini blinds. The storm was passing. Good. He didn't like the idea of Rainy driving through heavy rain and hail, even if the storm was mild.

The overhead lights flickered once—no big deal after a rainstorm.

He buttoned his shirt and reached for dry boots. A deafening crash rattled the windows. The boots clattered to the floor. He yanked the door open and rushed into the living room. Pop, Emma and Will, all wearing identical stunned expressions, met him there.

"What was that?" he asked, taking in the saucer-sized eyes of the two children.

"Don't know," Pop said. "Lightning maybe?"

"Maybe, though the storm is letting up," Nate said. "Struck close by, I'd say."

"Yeah. Real close." Pop relayed a silent message.

Nate nodded. "I'd better check outside. Make sure the animals and barns are okay." Lightning on a hay barn could cause a mean fire in a hurry. He glanced at the children. "Where's Joshua?"

"He was right there a minute ago," Will pointed toward the window. "Watching the hail."

"Joshua?" Nate called. No answer.

His expression worried, Will ran toward the bathroom but returned in a second's time. "He's not in there."

A tingle of fear prickled the hair on Nate's neck. Joshua was not afraid of storms. He was not hiding in the back of the closet.

"If he's not in the house, where is he?" Pop asked.

"The hail," Will said softly, eyes growing even wider. "He wanted to get some hail when the rain stopped. To measure it."

At that moment, a high-pitched wail lifted above the conversation, and Nate knew.

"Oh no." He was in a dead run before he reached the front door.

The big cedar tree next to the driveway angled across the front yard, split at the trunk. Beneath it was Joshua.

His heart hammering in his ears, Nate rushed to the fallen child. Water soaked his socks. As he stumbled to his knees in the wet grass, Pop, Will and Emma came up behind.

Emma set up a wail. "Joshie's hurt."

"Hush, child," Pop said, patting the top of her blond head, though his concern focused on the cedar-trapped boy. "Josh boy, where are you hurt?"

"I—I—I don't know," Joshua's voice was thin and shaky. "The tree is smashing me. I can't get out."

Nate pushed at the prickly cedar branches, sliding his hand over the wet, rough grass, until he touched Joshua's foot. "Hang on, buddy. We'll have you out in a minute. I'll move the tree, and Pop will pull you out. Okay?"

While listening for Joshua's wobbly agreement, he signaled a silent message to his granddad. *The boy could have broken bones. Take it easy.* Pop responded with a nod.

As Nate put a shoulder to the enormous old cedar, Will appeared, adding his slight weight to the effort. Nate was proud of him for that. Later, he'd let him know.

With muscles quivering, they lifted the splintered cedar a few inches, enough for Pop to gently ease Joshua into the clear. The boy began to cry.

Thunder rumbled overhead and the sky had darkened again.

"Let's get him inside." With great care, Nate scooped the shivering child into his arms. Joshua's back was as soaked as Nate socks.

Once in the house, he gently placed Joshua on the sofa and began to assess the damage. Scratches on his face and arms. A bruise on his shoulder, which appeared to have taken the brunt of the falling limb. Nothing looked permanent or serious. Thank God. He couldn't bear for anything terrible to happen to one of Rainy's kids.

Keeping his own rampaging emotions under control, he said softly, "What happened out there, Joshua?"

Joshua's lips trembled as tears slid along the side of his nose and into the corners of his mouth. "I don't know. I went to grab some hail. I thought the storm was over. Then I heard a big boom and the tree hit me."

The child rotated his shoulder, touching it gingerly with his opposite hand.

"Lightning must have struck it," Pop said.

A tremor of horror was replaced by more gratitude as Nate realized how close the boy had come to a life-and-death situation. Thanks to a merciful, loving God, the lightning had not struck Joshua.

"Is he all right?" Will hovered next to the couch, his face white and pinched. Emma stood at one end, stroking Joshua's hair over and over again.

"Looks like he will be. He's one tough cowboy, aren't you,

Joshua? He can take on a bolt of lightning and a giant cedar tree and come out the winner." Nate winked at the shaking child. "I don't find any broken bones, but Miss Rainy may want to have you checked out by the doctor."

Will crumpled to the floor and thrust his face against his upraised knees. His glasses pushed to one side at an odd angle. "I'm sorry, Joshua. I'm sorry. I shouldn't have let you go."

By now, Pop had brought a damp cloth and was carefully cleaning Joshua's scratches as he checked for more injuries.

Nate turned his attention to Will.

"Whoa, now. What's this all about? Little brother will be fine."

"I knew he wanted to go out there. I shouldn't have let him. It's my fault he got hurt."

Nate sat down on the floor beside the older child and draped an arm over the shaking shoulders. "Will, that's not true. This is not your fault. Joshua did what he did. You can't take the blame for his actions."

"I'm supposed to take care of him."

"No, you aren't. That is not your job, Will."

The boy raised his head and looked at Nate with red, guilt-ridden eyes. He shoved angrily at his dirty glasses. "I'm the big brother. It *is* my job."

The big brother. Guilt-ridden and overresponsible.

Nate felt as if he'd been hit in the gut with a ball bat. Hadn't he said these same words a thousand times? Hadn't he walked in Will's shoes?

"No, son. No."

He squeezed his eyes shut and pulled Will against his side. None of this was Will's fault but the boy carried the burden for all of his siblings. Just as Nate did.

Dear Lord, have I been wrong all this time?

While he sat on the hardwood floor consoling the child,

the telephone rang. He patted Will's shoulder. "Hang tight, my man. I'll be back."

Pop waved him off. "You look after the kids. I'll get the phone."

Nate urged Will to his feet. Keeping his hands on Will's shoulders, Nate scooted both of them onto the couch next to Joshua. "See, buddy, he's all right. Aren't you, Joshua?"

Rubbing at a long scratch on his cheek, the younger brother nodded. Just then, Pop hollered from the kitchen. "Blake's on the horn. Wants to talk to you."

Instead of the usual leap of worry that something terrible had happened to his brother, something new and unfamiliar passed over Nate. Truth. Freedom. "Ask him if it's an emergency."

A grin twitched Pop's mouth. "Only to him. He forgot to pay his cell phone bill. Six hundred dollars."

"Six hundred—" Nate caught himself. He was the big brother. He should take care of it. For the first time in his life, he recognized the lie behind those words.

As clearly as if the clouds had disappeared and the sun illuminated a path, Nate recognized the parallel between his mind-set and Will's. They were both wrong. He was no more responsible for his brother and sister than Will was to blame for Joshua's accident.

"Tell him he's on his own." Nate stilled himself against an onslaught of guilt. It never came. "From now on."

Pop blinked at him in wonder before a slow, satisfied smile spread across his weathered face. He spoke into the receiver for several more minutes, then disconnected and returned to the living room where he clapped a broad hand on Nate's shoulder.

"I don't know what brought that on, Nate boy, but all I can say is it's about time."

All these years, he'd blamed himself, carried the burden of familial responsibility that was not his to carry. As a result, the things he'd done for his siblings were out of guilt and fear, not love, and as Rainy had tried to tell him, he'd hurt them more than helped them. He'd made them weak and dependent.

He'd failed. Not because he hadn't tried hard enough or done enough, but because he'd left God out of the equation, thinking he had to handle everything on his own.

He gathered Rainy's three children into his arms, recognizing the love he'd been holding back.

"God help me," he muttered. "I have been a foolish man."

Part of faith was being able to give the things and the people he loved to God and trust that the God who made the universe could care for them far better than one guilt-ridden cowboy.

Rainy couldn't figure out what was going on in Nate's head. He'd followed her to the A.M.-P.M. Clinic to have Joshua's shoulder X-rayed, adding support, looking after Emma and Will in the waiting room, and generally behaving as if he'd never shut her out of his life.

By the time she arrived at her house, it was nearly ten o'clock. The kids were exhausted and emotionally overwrought, but thankfully, Joshua's shoulder was only sprained and bruised. As a foster parent, she'd had other close calls, but this one was the most serious. She was so glad Nate and Pop had been present when the accident occurred. The kids loved and trusted them. So did she.

She sneaked a glance at the tall, perplexing cowboy. As if it were the most natural thing in the world, he was sitting on the edge of Will's twin bed, talking in low tones. She couldn't hear what was being said, but Will's serious mind was taking everything in.

Across the room, she helped Joshua into his Scooby pajama top, being careful of the bruised arm. Then she tucked him into bed.

"You have a lot to be thankful for tonight, Joshua," she said as she kissed his soap-scented forehead.

"Yeah. A lot." His big blue eyes looked from her to Nate and Will and then tiredly closed.

After a heartfelt prayer of thanks for his safety, which Rainy silently affirmed, he said, "Thank You, too, for Nate. I'm glad he was there to take care of me. I think I love him, Jesus. I wouldn't mind having him for a dad."

Rainy's eyes flew open. She glanced across at Nate, but the cowboy apparently hadn't heard. Thank goodness. He'd made himself clear on that subject.

"And Jesus—" Joshua went on, heedless of the turmoil he'd initiated "—please bless my brother. Tell him it wasn't his fault. I was the dummy who went outside. Okay, I'm done now. Thank you. Amen."

Rainy stood, gazing down at the beautiful boy. "I love you, Joshua."

A tiny smile appeared as his lids drooped.

"I love you…" Before he could finish the thought, Joshua was asleep.

Rainy pushed the damp hair away from his forehead and kissed him again before leaving the room.

Emma had fallen asleep on the ride home and was already in bed. Rainy rubbed weary hands over her face and through her hair. What an evening.

She had two cups of hot chocolate in the microwave when Nate came out of the boys' bedroom. Back turned to the cabinets, she heard his boots *tap-tapping* on the tile. Maybe now she could find out what was going on with him tonight.

As she removed a bag of marshmallows from a shelf, her own smiley-face puppet appeared over her shoulder.

"Hey, Slick," the puppet said in Nate's voice. "How you doing?"

Touched, amused, she leaned her cheek against the puppet

for a brief moment, fully aware that Nate's hand was the recipient of her affection. "Tired, but thankful. How about you, Mr. Smiley?"

There was a pause before Mr. Smiley slid away. Rainy felt the loss clear to her tired feet.

"I'm sorry Joshua was injured on my watch," Nate said.

Rainy slowly turned around. Nate was standing inches away, his eyes darkened with emotion, the smiley puppet dangling at his side.

"You can't watch them every second. They're boys. Boys are adventurers. Don't blame yourself."

"I'm not."

"That's a first."

"Yeah, it is."

He looked as weary as she felt, his hair disheveled and his shirt smudged with dirt and smelling of cedar sap. Yet an aura of peace emanated from him such as she'd never seen before.

Something was going on with Nate Del Rio. Something good. A ray of foolish hope energized her.

"Is Will all right?" she asked, stirring the cocoa. "Joshua mentioned that he thought he was somehow to blame for the accident."

The reaction was typical of Will. He carried the burden of his brother and sister as seriously as Nate did.

The parallel had occurred to her before.

Rubbing a hand over the top of his hair, mussing the brown stuff even more, Nate nodded. "I straightened him out about that."

He had? Mister I'm-Responsible-for-the-World had straightened out Will's similar thinking?

She handed over a mug filled with hot cocoa and floating with marshmallows. "How did you do that?"

Eager to rest her weary body, Rainy led the way into the living room, where she curled her feet beneath her on one end of the couch. Nate perched on the edge at the other end, his elbows on knees, the cup in both hands. The puppet lay inert between them, its wide eyes and permanent smile looking up at them with happy interest.

"I told him about me," he said, studying the rising steam from his cocoa. "About how I'd been wrong for a long time and didn't know it. About how he and the Lord had opened my eyes today."

Rainy blew across the top of her mug. "I'm afraid you've lost me."

He looked up then, caught her gaze with his and held on. "I hope not. With everything in me, I hope I haven't lost you."

Rainy's heart skipped a beat. What was he saying? That he was sorry for the break up? That he cared? She tilted her head as the ember of hope became a flame. "Nate? What's going on?"

"I was wrong, Rainy. About us. About Janine and Blake. About everything." He set the cup aside. "I love those kids in there."

"I know you do." She'd always known. No matter how he denied the emotion, everything he did screamed love.

His jaw worked for a few seconds. His nostrils flared.

"I love you, too."

The beautiful words floated across the space like colorful balloons in a blue, blue sky. Rainy's throat filled with emotion. She wasn't sure what had transpired, but she was too happy to care.

She smiled. "Feeling's mutual, Cowboy."

He squeezed his eyes closed for one brief moment, shaking his head. "I don't deserve you, but if you can forgive me, if you can give me another chance, I promise to do things a lot differently this time."

Nate rose and took the cocoa cup from her hands, setting it next to his on the coffee table. Kneeling before her on one knee, his fingers, warm from the hot drink, entwined with hers.

"So what do you think? Will you give this dumb cowboy another try?"

Rainy studied his beloved face, soaking him in. As much as she loved him, he had to understand one important thing. She wouldn't back away from the calling God had placed on her life to minister to children. Not even for him.

Nate jiggled her hand. "Help me out here, Slick. You're too quiet."

"I come with baggage, Nate. You know that. God willing, I'm going to adopt those three in there. And I'll go right on taking in foster children as long as God wants me to."

"Wouldn't it be easier if you had a partner to help out?"

She was almost afraid to believe this was for real. "I can't settle for any old partner, Nate. Only someone who loves these kids and is as committed to them as I am."

Nate picked up Mr. Smiley, working his giant, grinning mouth.

"I know a guy like that," Mr. Smiley said. "Good-looking dude. Owns a ranch. Crazy about you. Crazy about your kids. Come on, Miss Rainy, what do you say? Throw the guy a bone."

Rainy grabbed the puppet, stopping the onslaught of words. "What happened to the cowboy who never wanted kids? The one who said kids are too much trouble?"

"Lightning struck. God spoke. I listened." He took her hand in his and squeezed gently. "I've been battling the idea for a long time. Ever since we met, I guess, and you pushed your way into my heart."

"I do not push." She bunched one shoulder. "Well, maybe a little."

"Like a velvet bulldozer." His killer dimples flashed. "After Katie was taken, I got cold feet, thinking I couldn't take the hurt. But today, when Joshua was under that tree, I realized I was going to love him no matter where he was. He might as well be with me as my son."

Tears pushed up behind Rainy's eyes. "Nate Del Rio, I love you so much. You big jerk."

He kissed her on the nose. "Did you just agree to marry me?"

"Did you just ask me to?"

A grin spread across his handsome features.

"Yep," he said in wonder. "I sure did."

Rainy traced the whisker-roughened jaw line, touched the firm crease of dimple next to his mouth. "Will you answer a question for me?"

"Anything. Anything you want. As long as you'll be in my life, I'll do anything."

"Why did you let the Pierson lease go?"

She could tell she'd shocked him. He rocked back on his heels. She tugged him back. "I saw the For Sale sign. I asked Pop and he said to ask you. So I'm asking."

"You don't need to know."

His answer told her everything. "You were my secret donor from the church, weren't you?"

"Your happiness is worth more to me than any piece of land ever could be."

So he'd sacrificed his dreams and every penny he'd saved for her and Katie and their lost cause.

"Oh, Nate. You wonderful, generous, incredible man. No wonder I fell madly in love with you."

She leaned forward and wrapped her arms around his neck. "You gave up your dream for me and Katie and got nothing in return."

With a tenderness that brought tears to her eyes, Nate cupped her face. "No, my darlin', you're wrong. I got everything a man could want."

Epilogue

Nate thought the courtroom looked the same. Cold. Austere. Formal. Only the atmosphere was different. Anticipatory. Happy.

He glanced at the woman snuggled close to his side on the hard wooden bench. His chest swelled with love for his bride of three months. She was nervous, but in a different way than on that terrible day of Katie's custody hearing. Glowing with excitement, Rainy fussed over first one child and then another until all three squirmed.

The kids looked perfect, like Easter portraits. Emma was princess gorgeous in a frilly yellow dress with white patent-leather shoes and ribbons in her hair. Will and Joshua looked as handsome and studious and neat as bankers in blue dress shirts and black slacks.

Nate couldn't hold back a grin at Will's pained expression, as the boy tugged at the necktie pressing his Adam's apple. Nate tugged at his own just for good measure. Will noticed and his eyes crinkled behind the plastic frames.

"When is the judge coming?" he whispered to Nate.

"Soon." Nate reassured his soon-to-be-son with a pat on the knee.

Son. Will would be his child forever. As would Joshua and Emma.

The wonder of it moved through him, as warm and cleansing as summer rain.

He could hardly believe the way his life had changed in the past year. On Valentine's Day, he and Rainy had married in a simple church ceremony filled with love and spirituality and family blessings. Then, with Pop happy to play granddad to the kids, the newlyweds had honeymooned in beautiful Cancun, a wedding gift from Rainy's parents.

Now, his once tidy, quiet ranch was lively with children and toys and schoolbooks, along with Miss Rainy's puppets and chocolate baking.

Kathy Underkircher and her bitter complaints had come to nothing. Thank God. Now Rainy and the children were safely away from her prying eyes and ears, a fact that gave him immense satisfaction.

Blake and Janine had been stunned when their older brother insisted on having a life of his own. To their credit, though they still struggled they were gaining ground, slowly becoming independent adults—and happier for the change. Last Sunday afternoon Janine and the baby had come for a visit and had left much later without requesting anything but Rainy's recipe for brownies.

With Rainy by his side and the Lord as his guide, Nate knew he would never go back to his self-imposed martyrdom.

"All please rise. This court is in session. Judge Bohannon presiding."

Rainy's fingers jerked in his and he winked at her.

The serious-looking judge scanned the gathered assembly, his gaze landing on Nate, Rainy and the children. Emma lifted a small hand and waved at the man. His responding chuckle relaxed them all.

In minutes, the proceedings were over. The judge offered

his congratulations and proclaimed Will, Joshua and Emma
to be the lawful children of Nate and Rainy Del Rio.

Before the black-robed jurist had swept from the courtroom, the three children erupted in celebration, hugging and
high-fiving everyone in sight. Even the social worker had
tears of happiness in her eyes.

Rainy threw herself into Nate's arms in exuberant joy.
With a laugh, he lifted her high into the air. As he settled her
to the earth again, three children attacked his legs. He and
Rainy formed a circle, embracing their sons and daughter.

"Grab a hand," he said, his voice gruff with emotion.

Over the months of bonding, the children had come to
understand. In a circle of family, they bowed their heads
while Nate quietly gave thanks, heart full enough to burst,
mere words inadequate.

Why had he ever thought he didn't want this? How could
he have ever been so blind?

When the prayer ended, Joshua looked up at Rainy. "Can
we tell him now, Miss Rainy?" He shook his head. "I mean,
Mom."

"Yeah, Mom," Will said, trying the name on for size.
"Let's tell Dad the news."

A quiver of something new and wonderful moved through
Nate. Dad. He was a dad.

"Yeah, Mom," Emma said, not to be outdone. "Tell Dad."

Man, he liked that word. Nate looked from one member
of his new family to the other. "Tell Dad what? Are you
already keeping secrets from the old man?"

Rainy's face was radiant. "A good secret. You're going to
like this. I promise."

She reached inside her purse and removed an envelope
which she handed to him. The kids gazed on, expectant,
smiling.

Nate turned the envelope over in his hands. "What is this?"

"Open it and see." By now, Rainy was jiggling up and down, as eager as a kid on Christmas.

He removed the legal-looking paper and quickly scanned it. He gazed up, bewildered. "This is a contract to buy the Pierson property."

"Mom bought it for you, Nate. I mean, Dad," Will said. "She bought it for our family."

"You couldn't have. How could you have?"

Rainy's sweet smile would stay with him forever. "When I put my house up for sale, I contacted Mr. Pierson, explained the situation, and convinced him to wait a little longer before selling to anyone else."

"Convinced him?" Yes, he could see that. His velvet bulldozer could persuade the feathers from a peacock.

"Then when my house sold," she went on, very pleased with herself, "he and I made the deal. My profit from the house easily covered the down payment on the land, with some left over for those cows you wanted to buy."

"I can't believe this." But he held the legal evidence in his hands. "You did this for me?"

"For you. For me. For all of us, cowboy. Your dreams are my dreams now."

He couldn't hold back. There on the front lawn of the courthouse surrounded by three giggling, whooping children, he pulled his beautiful bride into his arms and kissed her.

As her warm, loving lips met his, Nate Del Rio lifted his heart to God in praise for the day a city slicker and her passel of children bulldozed their way into his life—

And made him like it.

* * * * *

Don't miss Linda Goodnight's next heartwarming romance when THE BABY BOND goes on sale in May 2009, only for Steeple Hill Love Inspired.

Dear Reader,

I'm often asked if I write myself into my stories. This is one book where I did, at least to a small degree. Like the heroine, Rainy, I love to bake, especially chocolate. Also like Rainy, I tend to bake when under stress. Below is the recipe for Rainy's (and my) favorite brownies. I hope you like them, too.

Rainy's Chocoholic Brownie Recipe

Melt 1/2 cup semisweet chocolate chips with 1 stick of butter or margarine. I do this in the microwave but you may also do it on the stovetop over low heat.

Stir in, mixing well after each addition:

1/4 cup flour
1/4 cup cocoa
1/2 cup brown sugar
1/2 cup sugar
2 eggs
1 tsp. vanilla
1/2 cup pecans or walnuts (optional)

Spread in a sprayed or greased 8x8 baking pan. Bake at 350 degrees for 40 minutes. To test for doneness, an inserted toothpick will come out crumbly-moist. Do not overbake.

Enjoy!

Linda Goodnight

QUESTIONS FOR DISCUSSION

1. According to his grandfather, Nate struggled with a "works mentality." What does this mean? Have you ever known anyone who thought they had to work their way into God's favor?

2. Discuss some of the ways Nate "worked" for God's favor. Did his efforts do him any good?

3. At one point, Pop reminds Nate that motive is everything. What did he mean by that? Is it possible to be a Christian and have a resentful heart?

4. Many Christians serve their churches or fellow man in some way. Is this the same as "works mentality"? Discuss the difference.

5. Nate says he never wants kids. Why does he feel that way? Are his feelings justified?

6. Rainy believes God has called her to be an adoptive parent even though she is single. What is your position on single-parent adoptions? Why? Are there any instances of adoption in the Bible?

7. Kathy Underkircher, Rainy's neighbor, causes problems for Rainy over a perceived slight. Was there anything else Rainy could have done as a Christian to win Kathy's approval? Should a Christian always turn the other cheek?

8. The foster child, Katie, is returned to her birth mother. How did you feel about that? Was this the best choice

for Katie? Is a birth parent always a better alternative than an adoptive one?

9. How is the word "Crossroads" in the title significant to the story? Discuss both types of crossroads in Nate's life.

10. Did any other characters experience a "crossroads" during the course of the book? Explain.

11. Nate suffered terrible guilt over the death of his sister. Do you think he was to blame in any way? Could he have prevented her death? Was he wrong in not responding to her call?

12. Do you think each person has an appointed time to die and nothing can prevent it? Or can the action of human beings determine matters of life and death? Whichever you choose, is there scripture to back up your beliefs?

13. Nate believes he isn't one of God's favorite people. Do you think God favors some Christians over others? Why or why not? Can you find scripture references concerning God's favor?

Turn the page for a sneak preview of bestselling author
Jillian Hart's novella
"Finally a Family"

One of two heartwarming stories
celebrating motherhood in
IN A MOTHER'S ARMS

On sale April 2009, only from
Steeple Hill Love Inspired Historical.

Chapter One

Montana Territory, 1884

Molly McKaslin sat in her rocking chair in her cozy little shanty with her favorite book in hand. The lush new-spring green of the Montana prairie spread out before her like a painting, framed by the wooden window. The blue sky was without a single cloud to mar it. Lemony sunshine spilled over the land and across the open window's sill. The door was wedged open, letting the outside noises in—the snap of laundry on the clothesline and the chomping crunch of an animal grazing. My, it sounded terribly close.

The peaceful afternoon quiet shattered with a crash. She leaped to her feet to see her good—and only—china vase splintered on the newly washed wood floor. She stared in shock at the culprit standing at her other window. A golden cow with a white blaze down her face poked her head further across the sill. The bovine gave a woeful moo. One look told her this was the only animal in the yard.

"And just what are you doing out on your own?" She set her book aside.

The cow lowed again. She was a small heifer, still probably more baby than adult. The cow lunged against the sill, straining toward the cookie racks on the table.

"At least I know how to catch you." She grabbed a cookie off the rack and the heifer's eyes widened. "I don't recognize you, so I don't think you belong here."

Molly skirted around the mess on the floor and headed toward the door. This was the consequence of agreeing to live in the country, when she had vowed never to do so again. But her path had led her to this opportunity, living on her cousin's land and helping the family. God had quite a sense of humor, indeed.

Before she could take two steps into the soft, lush grass surrounding her shanty, the cow came running, head down, big brown eyes fastened on the cookie. The ground shook.

Uh oh. Molly's heart skipped two beats.

"No, Sukie, no!" High, girlish voices carried on the wind.

Molly briefly caught sight of two identical school-aged girls racing down the long dirt road. The animal was too single-minded to respond. She pounded the final few yards, her gaze fixed on the cookie.

"Stop, Sukie. Whoa." Molly kept her voice low and kindly firm. She knew cows responded to kindness better than to anything else. She also knew they were not good at stopping, so she dropped the cookie on the ground and neatly stepped out of the way. The cow skidded well past the cookie and the place where Molly had been standing.

"It's right here." She showed the cow where the oatmeal treat was resting in the clean grass. While the animal backed up and nipped up the goody, Molly grabbed the cow's rope halter.

"Good. She didn't stomp you into bits." One of the girls said in serious relief. "She ran me over real good just last week."

"We thought you were a goner," the second girl said. "She's real nice, but she doesn't see very well."

"She sees well enough to have found me." Molly studied the girls. They both had identical black braids and golden-hazel eyes and fine-boned porcelain faces. One twin wore a green calico dress with matching sunbonnet, while the other wore blue. She recognized the girls from church and around town. " Aren't you the doctor's children?"

"Yep, that's us." The first girl offered a beaming, dimpled smile. "I'm Penelope and that's Prudence. We're real glad you found Sukie."

"We wouldn't want a cougar to get her."

"Or a bear."

What adorable children. A faint scattering of freckles dappled across their sun-kissed noses, and there was a glint of trouble in their eyes as the twins looked at one another. The place in her soul thirsty for a child of her own ached painfully. She felt hollow and empty, as if her body would always remember carrying the baby she had lost. For one moment it was as if the wind died and the earth vanished.

"Hey, what is she eating?" One of the girls tumbled forward. "It smells like a cookie. You are a bad girl, Sukie."

"Did she walk into your house and eat off the counter?" Penelope wanted to know.

The grass crinkled beneath her feet as the cow tugged her toward the girls. "No, she went through the window."

Penelope went up on tiptoe. "I see them. They look real good."

Molly gazed down at their sweet and innocent faces. She wasn't fooled. Then again, she was a soft touch. "I'll see what I can do."

She headed back inside. "Do you girls need help getting the cow home?"

"No. She's real tame." Penelope and the cow trailed after her, hesitating outside the door. "We can lead her anywhere."

"Yeah, she only runs off when she's looking for us."

"Thank you so much, Mrs.—" Penelope took the napkin-wrapped stack of cookies. "We don't know your name."

"This is the McKaslin ranch," Prudence said thoughtfully. "But I know you're not Mrs. McKaslin."

"I'm the cousin. I moved here this last winter. You can call me Molly."

Penelope gave her twin a cookie. Beneath the brim of her sunbonnet, her face crinkled with serious thought. "You don't know our pa yet?"

"No, I only know Dr. Frost by reputation. I hear he's a fine doctor." That was all she knew. Of course she had seen his fancy black buggy speeding down the country roads at all hours. Sometimes she caught a brief sight of the man driving as the horse-drawn vehicle passed—an impression of a black Stetson, a strong granite profile and impressively wide shoulders.

Although she was on her own and free to marry, she paid little heed to eligible men. All she knew of Doctor Sam Frost was that he was a widower and a father and a faithful man, for he often appeared very serious in church. She reached through the open door to where her coats hung on wall pegs and worked the sash off her winter wool.

Prudence smiled. "Our pa's real nice and you make good cookies."

"And you're real pretty." Penelope was so excited she didn't notice Sukie stealing her cookie. "Do you like Pa?"

"I don't know the man, so I can't like him. I suppose I can't dislike him, either." She bent to secure the sash around Sukie's halter. "Let me walk you girls across the road."

"You ought to come home with us." Penelope grinned. "Then you can meet Pa."

"Do you want to get married?" Penelope's feet were planted.

So were Prudence's. "Yes! You could marry Pa. Do you want to?"

"M-marry your pa?" Shock splashed over her like icy water.

"Sure. You could be our ma."

"And then Pa wouldn't be so lonely anymore."

Molly blinked. The words were starting to sink in. The poor girls, wishing so much for a mother that they would take any stranger who was kind to them. "No, I certainly cannot marry a perfect stranger, but thank you for asking. I would take you two in a heartbeat."

"You would?" Penelope looked surprised. "Really?"

"We're an awful lot of trouble. Our housekeeper said that three times today since church."

"Does your pa know you propose on his behalf?"

"Now he does." A deep baritone answered. Dr. Frost marched into sight, rounding the corner of the shanty. His hat brim shaded his face, casting shadows across his chiseled features, giving him an even more imposing appearance. "Girls! Home! Not another word."

"But we had to save Sukie."

"She could have been eaten by a wolf."

Molly watched the good doctor's mouth twitch. She couldn't be sure, but a flash of humor could have twinkled in the depths of his eyes.

"You must be the cousin." He swept off his hat. The twinkle faded from his eyes and the hint of a grin from his lips. It was clear that while his daughters amused him, she did not. "I had no idea you would be so young."

"And pretty," Penelope, obviously the troublemaker, added mischievously.

Molly's face heated. The poor girl must need glasses. Although Molly was still young, time and sadness had made its mark on her. The imposing man had turned into granite as he faced her. Of course he had overheard his daughters' proposal, so that might explain it.

She smiled and took a step away from him. "Dr. Frost, I'm

glad you found your daughters. I was about ready to bring them back to you."

"I'll save you the trouble." He didn't look happy. "Girls, take that cow home. I need to stay and apologize to Miss McKaslin."

She was a "Mrs." but she didn't correct him. She had put away her black dresses and her grief. Her marriage had mostly been a long string of broken dreams. She did better when she didn't remember. "Please don't be too hard on the girls on my behalf. Sukie's arrival livened up my day."

"At least there was no harm done." He winced. "There was harm? What happened?"

"I didn't say a word."

"No, but I could see it on your face."

Had he been watching her so closely? Or had she been so unguarded? Perhaps it was his closeness. She could see bronze flecks in his gold eyes, and smell the scents of soap and spring clinging to his shirt. A spark of awareness snapped within her like a candle newly lit. "It was a vase. Sukie knocked it off my windowsill when she tried to eat the flowers, but it was an accident."

"The girls should take better care of their pet." He drew his broad shoulders into an unyielding line. He turned to check on the twins, who were progressing down the road. The wind ruffled his dark hair. He seemed distant. Lost. "How much was the vase worth?"

How did she tell him it was without price? Perhaps it would be best not to open that door to her heart. "It was simply a vase."

"No, it was more." He stared at his hat clutched in both hands. "Was it a gift?"

"No, it was my mother's."

"And is she gone?"

"Yes."

"Then I cannot pay you its true value. I'm sorry." His gaze met hers with startling intimacy. Perhaps a door was open to his heart, as well, because sadness tilted his eyes. He looked like a man with many regrets.

She knew well the weight of that burden. "Please, don't worry about it."

"The girls will replace it." His tone brooked no argument, but it wasn't harsh. "About what my daughters said to you."

"Do you mean their proposal? Don't worry. It's plain to see they are simply children longing for a mother's love."

"Thank you for understanding. Not many folks do."

"Maybe it's because I know something about longing. Life never turns out the way you plan it."

"No. Life can hand you more sorrow than you can carry." Although he did not move a muscle, he appeared changed. Stronger, somehow. Greater. "I'm sorry the girls troubled you, Miss McKaslin."

Mrs., but again she didn't correct him. It was the sorrow she carried that stopped her from it. She preferred to stand in the present with sunlight on her face. "It was a pleasure, Dr. Frost. What blessings you have in those girls."

"That I know." He tipped his hat to her, perhaps a nod of respect, and left her alone with the restless wind and the door still open in her heart.

* * * * *

Don't miss IN A MOTHER'S ARMS
Featuring two brand-new novellas from bestselling authors
Jillian Hart and Victoria Bylin.
Available April 2009
from Steeple Hill Love Inspired Historical.

And be sure to look for SPRING CREEK BRIDE
by Janice Thompson,
also available in April 2009.

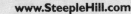

Love Inspired

Everyone in Mule Hollow can see the resemblance between former Texas Ranger Zane Cantrell and Rose Vincent's son. Zane is in shock—how could Rose have kept such a secret from him? Rose reminds Zane that *he's* the one who walked away. Zane needs to convince her he had had no choice... and that's when the matchmaking begins.

Look for

Texas Ranger Dad

by

Debra Clopton

Available April
wherever books are sold.

REQUEST YOUR FREE BOOKS!

2 FREE INSPIRATIONAL NOVELS
PLUS 2
FREE
MYSTERY GIFTS

YES! Please send me 2 FREE Love Inspired® novels and my 2 FREE mystery gifts (gifts are worth about $10). After receiving them, if I don't wish to receive any more books, I can return the shipping statement marked "cancel". If I don't cancel, I will receive 4 brand-new novels every month and be billed just $4.24 per book in the U.S. or $4.74 per book in Canada, plus 25¢ shipping and handling per book and applicable taxes, if any*. That's a savings of over 20% off the cover price! I understand that accepting the 2 free books and gifts places me under no obligation to buy anything. I can always return a shipment and cancel at any time. Even if I never buy another book, the two free books and gifts are mine to keep forever.

113 IDN ERXA 313 IDN ERWX

Name	(PLEASE PRINT)	
Address		Apt. #
City	State/Prov.	Zip/Postal Code
Signature (if under 18, a parent or guardian must sign)		

Order online at www.LoveInspiredBooks.com

Or mail to Steeple Hill Reader Service:

IN U.S.A.: P.O. Box 1867, Buffalo, NY 14240-1867
IN CANADA: P.O. Box 609, Fort Erie, Ontario L2A 5X3

Not valid to current subscribers of Love Inspired books.

Want to try two free books from another series?
Call 1-800-873-8635 or visit www.morefreebooks.com

* Terms and prices subject to change without notice. N.Y. residents add applicable sales tax. Canadian residents will be charged applicable provincial taxes and GST. Offer not valid in Quebec. This offer is limited to one order per household. All orders subject to approval. Credit or debit balances in a customer's account(s) may be offset by any other outstanding balance owed by or to the customer. Please allow 4 to 6 weeks for delivery. Offer available while quantities last.

Your Privacy: Steeple Hill Books is committed to protecting your privacy. Our Privacy Policy is available online at www.SteepleHill.com or upon request from the Reader Service. From time to time we make our lists of customers available to reputable third parties who may have a product or service of interest to you. If you would prefer we not share your name and address, please check here. ☐

LIREG08R

Love Inspired®

TITLES AVAILABLE NEXT MONTH
Available March 31, 2009

TWICE UPON A TIME by Lois Richer
Weddings by Woodwards

Between his work and his twin boys, widower Reese Woodward
has no time for love. Or so he thinks until he meets Olivia Hastings,
his sister's best friend. Her past makes her wary of romance, but
who can resist the adorable twins—or their father? Together they
might find their second chance for a doubly blessed happy-ever-
after.

TEXAS RANGER DAD by Debra Clopton
A Mule Hollow Novel

When Texas Ranger Zane Cantrell returns to Mule Hollow after
years away, he comes face-to-face with the son of an old girlfriend—
who also happens to be his son! Zane can't believe Rose Vincent
kept this secret from him all these years. But he's eager to get to
know his boy, and to prove he's never stopped loving Rose. Can
they build a brand-new life together?

HOMECOMING BLESSINGS by Merrillee Whren

Small-town girl Amelia Hiatt and big-city businessman Peter Dalton
think they have nothing in common. When they team up on a
special project, they soon realize they're more alike than they could
ever imagine. Except the big-city bachelor isn't ready to settle down,
and Amelia is ready for a family of her own. But she's determined
to change his mind—and his heart.

READY-MADE FAMILY by Cheryl Wyatt
Wings of Refuge

Ben Dillinger is used to playing the hero to damsels in distress, he's
just not used to falling in love with them! When the pararescue
jumper rescues single mom Amelia North and her daughter from
a car accident, Ben realizes he's found the family he's been longing
for. And he'll do whatever it takes to prove to her that he's the
missing piece in her ready-made family.

LICNMBPA0309